Dear Reader,

I just wanted to tell you how delighted I am that my publisher has decided to reprint so many of my earlier books. Some of them have not been available for a while, and amongst them there are titles that have often been requested.

I can't remember a time when I haven't written, although it was not until my daughter was born that I felt confident enough to attempt to get anything published. With my husband's encouragement, my first book was accepted, and since then there have been over 130 more.

Not that the thrill of having a book published gets any less. I still feel the same excitement when a new manuscript is accepted. But it's you, my readers, to whom I owe so much. Your support—and particularly your letters—give me so much pleasure.

I hope you enjoy this collection of some of my favourite novels.

Back by Popular Demand

With a phenomenal one hundred and thirty books published by Mills & Boon, Anne Mather is one of the world's most popular romance authors. Mills & Boon are proud to bring back many of these highly sought-after novels in a special collector's edition.

ANNE MATHER: COLLECTOR'S EDITION

1 JAKE HOWARD'S WIFE
2 SCORPIONS' DANCE
3 CHARADE IN WINTER
4 A FEVER IN THE BLOOD
5 WILD ENCHANTRESS
6 SPIRIT OF ATLANTIS
7 LOREN'S BABY
8 DEVIL IN VELVET
9 LIVING WITH ADAM
10 SANDSTORM
11 A HAUNTING COMPULSION
12 IMAGES OF LOVE
13 FALLEN ANGEL
14 TRIAL OF INNOCENCE
15 THE MEDICI LOVER
16 THE JUDAS TRAP
17 PALE ORCHID
18 CAROLINE
19 THE SHROUDED WEB
20 A TRIAL MARRIAGE

DEVIL IN VELVET

BY
ANNE MATHER

MILLS & BOON®

All the characters in this book have no existence outside the imagina-
tion of the author, and have no relation whatsoever to anyone bearing
the same name or names. They are not even distantly inspired by any
individual known or unknown to the author, and all the incidents are
pure invention.

First published in Great Britain 1977 by Mills & Boon Limited
This edition 1997
Harlequin Mills & Boon Limited,
Eton House, 18-24 Paradise Road, Richmond, Surrey TW9 1SR

© Anne Mather 1977

ISBN 0 263 80558 1

Set in Times Roman 11 on 12 pt by
Rowland Phototypesetting Limited
Bury St Edmunds, Suffolk

74-9712-46369

Made and printed in Great Britain by
Caledonian International Book Manufacturing Ltd, Glasgow

CHAPTER ONE

THE door wasn't locked, so she didn't need the key, and as she pushed it wide, the sickly-sweet odour of dampness and decay, and what might have been rotting apples, assailed her nostrils. A wooden table flanked by wooden benches and a disreputable old rocking chair near the hearth was the only furniture she could see, and a chipped enamel sink was surmounted by the kind of pumping mechanism she had thought obsolete for years. The stone floor was littered with leaves and other debris, blown in through the open gaps in the window, no doubt, and an ominous scuttering in the corner seemed to signify squatters of another species. Considering the heat outside, the air was cool, and her shirt which had been sticking to her back now sent a shiver of chill along her spine. The huge blackened hole of the fireplace had not even been swept clean before the last tenants departed, and the ashes from the grate had filmed everything with a fine grey dust.

Harriet's heart sank. How could they possibly stay here? The place was filthy, and damp; and what was that rustling sound she could hear? Rats? Involuntarily, she shifted from one foot to the other, suppressing a desire to wrap the flared cuffs of her trousers about her ankles. Where was the spotless furnished farmhouse she had expected? The white-painted retreat, set in the lush valley of the Dordogne, the land overflowing with wine and *pâté de foie gras*, as the brochure extravagantly put it? How could anyone sell this as a suitable dwelling place, when it resembled nothing so much as a derelict? Her temper rose. How *dared* anyone sell such a place—and to her!

She had left Susan in the car, but now she heard the girl's footsteps on the path behind her, and turning to face her endeavoured to disguise a little of the rage and frustration that was gripping her. Susan had had enough to stand these past weeks. Harriet hoped the sight of this place would not undo all the good work that had been done. It had seemed such a good idea, bringing her niece to France for a couple of months, giving her a completely new change of scene. Charles, Harriet's employer, had been so kind, giving her the time off like this. But practically all Harriet's savings had gone on this place. She had relied on the Paris agent's assurances that this farmhouse in Rochelac was exactly what she wanted; and now to find that this was not so was the most bitter kind of humiliation.

'Well?' Susan's young voice was reassuringly bright. 'Is this the place?'

Harriet allowed a small sigh to escape her. 'Unfortunately,' she conceded.

'Unfortunately?' Susan brushed past her to stand inside the door. 'Why unfortunately?'

'*Why?*' Harriet gazed at her incredulously. Then she waved an expressive arm. 'Need you ask?'

Susan shrugged. 'It is dirty,' she agreed, with the casual gift for understatement of a fourteen-year-old. 'But that doesn't matter, does it? I mean, we can soon clean it up.'

'It's damp!' retorted Harriet flatly. 'Can't you see those patches on the walls? I dread to think what it's like upstairs. As for the furniture. . .'

'Have you looked around?' enquired Susan, crossing the floor, apparently unperturbed by the possible presence of their unwelcome visitors, and opening a door which hitherto Harriet had taken little notice of. 'Hmm, this must be the parlour. Is that what it's called in France?'

'The *salon*,' replied Harriet automatically, staring bleakly about her. 'Susan, do mind where you're putting your feet. I heard scufflings when I came in.'

'Field mice probably,' called Susan airily. 'They always invade empty houses. Where are the stairs?'

'Oh, Susan, I don't know.' Harriet heaved another sigh, and looked round. 'I wonder who—' She broke off abruptly. 'It's my own fault, I suppose. I should have insisted on seeing this place before spending a penny. Wait until I lay my hands on Monsieur Frond! I doubt if he's ever been further south than Orleans!'

Susan came back into the kitchen. 'Why are you getting so upset, Harry? There's quite a decent pair of armchairs in there, and a sort of dresser. It's not the end of the world. I think it's rather super. You can see the garden at the back of the house, and there's actually a stream. . .'

'I imagine it's overgrown with weeds, too. The garden, I mean. And don't call me Harry!'

Susan grinned, the freckles on her face standing out against its pallor. These past weeks had robbed her of what little colour she had had, and it was good to see her smiling again. If the house could do that for her, it couldn't be all bad.

'Well, you don't like me calling you Aunt Harriet, do you?' she was saying now, and Harriet's features relaxed.

'No, that's true. But I'd prefer it if you called me plain Harriet instead of the abbreviation.'

'All right. Plain Harriet, it shall be,' teased Susan mischievously, and they both laughed. 'Seriously, though,' she went on, 'it's not so bad, is it? I like it. I'm sick of—conventional things.'

Her voice quavered a little, and to give her a moment to recover herself, Harriet essayed a determined interest in her surroundings. There were other doors, and with some trepidation she opened one of them, relieved to find a wooden stairway winding to the upper floor.

'The stairs!' she announced dryly, and taking a deep breath, began to climb up.

There was no handrail, and they were very steep, and any notion of carpeting them would have to be abandoned. But at least they seemed sound enough. They emerged into a square apartment with a ceiling that sloped sharply towards tiny windows set under the eaves, and a floor that was rough with knots and uneven boards. There was a sagging bedstead, and a rag mat, and near the windows was a rickety old washstand with a cracked jug and basin. The smell of rotting fruit was stronger here, and the heat of the sun had robbed the room of all air, giving it a stuffy oppressive atmosphere.

The windows would all be intact here, thought Harriet cynically, but when she tried to open them they resisted all her efforts. The fact that it was cleaner up here registered only faintly as she fought with swollen woodwork.

Susan had followed her up and now exclaimed excitedly: 'Look! There must be a loft. There's a trapdoor.'

Harriet looked round half impatiently, looping her long pale hair back behind her ears with a careless hand. Susan was pointing to a square-shaped opening set into the crumbling plaster of the ceiling, and now Harriet noticed a wooden ladder propped against the wall beside the bed. Leaving the stubborn window, she came to stand below the trapdoor, but vetoed Susan's eagerness to explore further.

Glancing at her watch, she said: 'It's almost a quarter to five. If we're to spend the night here, and I'm not at all sure that we should, we ought to be making an effort towards tidying up downstairs.'

Susan stared at her. 'You're not thinking of leaving!'

'Not that exactly.' Harriet spoke slowly. 'But you must admit, Sue, it isn't exactly what we expected.'

'I don't mind.'

'You say that—'

'I mean it,' Susan interrupted her. 'It's a sort of adventure, really. And I've slept in worse places. Heavens, when I went camping with the Guides—'

'Well, I certainly didn't spend several thousand francs on a house that's only fit to camp in!' declared Harriet firmly, and then seeing Susan's face beginning to crumple, added quickly: 'Perhaps we can do something about it, but for tonight I think we should find a *pension* and stay there until I've had a chance to contact Monsieur Frond—'

'But we planned to camp here!' Susan pursed her lips. 'We've brought our sleeping bags.'

'Because I expected the beds might need airing,' Harriet reminded her, gesturing behind them. 'As you can see, there's only one bed, and I wouldn't allow a dog to sleep on that mattress! Besides, the air up here is foul, and until we can get those windows open. . .'

Ignoring the lost look that came into Susan's eyes, she clattered down the stairs again, her cork soles echoing hollowly on the treads, and emerged into the infinitely fresher atmosphere of the kitchen.

Susan followed her and together they surveyed the room. 'You have to admit—it is deplorable!' Harriet insisted, and Susan hunched her shoulders.

'Where are we going to stay then? And what will you say when you speak to Monsieur Frond?'

Harriet shook her head. She didn't honestly know herself. Had she any redress? She doubted it. She should have investigated the property beforehand, and not allowed herself to be duped by fairytale fantasies of vineyards and chateaux, and lazy afternoons punting along the river with an unlimited supply of Dubonnet.

'I don't know what I shall do,' she said now, noticing how the dust had already soiled her shirt. She stepped gingerly across the flagged floor and emerged into the sunlight breathing deeply, and unfastened another button to reveal a depth of cleavage she would never have dared display at home.

The car was parked in the lane, beyond the thorny hedge that marked the garden. It was certainly peaceful enough, and approaching down a tree-shaded avenue she had been as enthusiastic as Susan. But even this front stretch of garden rioted heedlessly, and what had seemed a simple enough task when she walked up the path, had now assumed larger proportions. The walls of the house needed painting, along with all its other shortcomings, she saw now, but she had allowed the wild roses and nasturtiums to blind her to that fact. She had scarcely noticed the knee-high grasses and choking bindweed, or the nettles that threatened to sting unwary legs.

'We will come back, won't we?' Susan demanded anxiously, as Harriet turned the key in the squeaking lock, and her aunt looked at her ruefully.

'We shall probably have to,' she conceded dryly. 'Or go home.'

Susan's lips trembled. 'You wouldn't—we couldn't do that, could we?'

Harriet gave a resigned grimace. 'Probably not,' she agreed. 'Come on, I'm thirsty. I think there's a can of lime juice in the car.'

Harriet felt tired and depressed now. She had been driving since early that morning, urged on by the eagerness to reach their destination. But it had all gone flat, and even her resentment towards Monsieur Frond was giving way to anger towards herself. When would she learn that people were not always what they seemed?

Sharing the can of lime juice with Susan, and assuming an interest she was far from feeling, she consulted the map, spreading it out over the steering wheel of the car, pinpointing their position with wry accuracy.

'Well, we're about thirty kilometres from Beynac, which I suppose is the nearest town, but the village is nearer, of course—Rochelac. Do you think we should try there?'

'Of course.' Obviously Susan preferred to stay

within a reasonable distance, and the village was only a matter of some three or four kilometres.

'There may not be a *pension* there,' Harriet observed thoughtfully, but Susan felt sure there would be. 'What if there's not?' asked Harriet reasonably, and her niece shrugged.

'We can always sleep in the car,' she pointed out, and unwillingly Harriet let her have her way.

To reach the village necessitated reversing back up the lane, it was too narrow to turn, and regaining the road that ran between two villages, Bel-sur-Baux and Rochelac. There was something vaguely familiar about Rochelac, which was what had attracted Harriet to it in the first place, but she didn't exactly know what it was.

From the road, it was possible to look down on the trees that surrounded the house. They were even able to see the grey tiles of the roof, and beyond, the shallow ravine where the stream tumbled. Distance lent enchantment, but Harriet was too tired and dishevelled to appreciate its finer points right then. Susan was less inhibited and looked back longingly, but her aunt pressed her foot down hard on the accelerator, and the small Fiat surged obediently forward.

Rochelac seemed to cling to the hillside above the river of which their stream was a tributary. Harriet guessed it might be possible to walk to the village as quickly as to drive the few kilometres round by the road, and then stifled the weakening thought. They would probably never find out, she told herself firmly, and there was no point in pretending otherwise.

The village was as picturesque as she could have wished: narrow streets, balconies overflowing with flowering creepers, a tiny square, and the inevitable spire of the church. Harriet parked the car outside a patisserie, where the smell of new bread was mouth-watering, and then locking the car she and Susan took a walk down the steep cobbled slope which led to the river.

The houses that flanked the stone jetty were tall and thin, jostling together as if to conserve space. Steep, pointed roofs thrust up against the rocky buttresses above, with jutting attic windows projecting at right angles. Here and there, colourful canvas blinds shielded the upper windows from the effects of sun on shining water, while the river flowed by, smooth and mysterious.

Susan stood at the very edge of the path and looked down into its depths, and Harriet came to join her, her eyes drawn by the enviable sight of a pleasure launch floating downstream, its passengers trailing wrists in the cooling water.

Then she heaved a deep sigh and said: 'Come along. We have to find somewhere to stay.'

'Oh, look!'

Susan had turned and was pointing beyond the village to where the turrets of a castle or a chateau, Harriet was never quite sure of the distinction, could be seen above the trees at the top of the escarpment. They had seen many such examples of architecture on their way to Rochelac, and had even taken the time to stop in Beynac and look at the castle which had once been the base of the sinister Mercadier. During the reign of Richard the Lionheart, he had pillaged the countryside around Beynac on behalf of the English king, until Simon de Montfort himself seized control in 1214. This area of France was rife with such stories, and its turbulent history was no small part of its attraction.

'Do you suppose anyone lives there?' asked Susan curiously, but Harriet could only shake her head.

'Your guess is as good as mine,' she replied. 'Let's walk up into the square again. There are no hotels or *pensions* down here.'

But the village appeared not to cater for passing tourists, and the proprietor of the only café explained that they did not get a lot of visitors. Fortunately Harriet was reasonably fluent in his language, her work having brought her to France on more than one occasion, as he explained that he only spoke a little English.

'So what now?' Harriet asked of Susan, trying not to show impatience with the girl. 'I don't honestly find the prospect of driving back to Beynac appealing.'

Susan grimaced, and addressed herself in school-girl French to the proprietor: '*Connaissez-vous quelqu'un qui pourrait nous héberger cette nuit?*'

The proprietor frowned, and then launched

into a long speech of which Susan understood little except the word *chateau*. She turned confused eyes in Harriet's direction, and taking pity on her, Harriet explained: 'Monsieur—er—Monsieur—?'

'Macon,' supplied the proprietor importantly, and smiling her thanks, Harriet continued: 'Monsieur Macon was saying that apart from the chateau, there are no houses large enough to accommodate visitors around here.'

'Is the chateau an hotel, then?' cried Susan excitedly, obviously finding the prospect of spending the night in some mediaeval castle to her liking, but Harriet quickly disillusioned her.

'Apparently no one lives in the chateau these days,' she said. 'The owner couldn't afford its upkeep, and it's fallen into disrepair like some other property I could mention. *Wait a minute*!'

This last was spoken with such vehemence that both Susan and Monsieur Macon started violently, and stared in bewilderment at Harriet, who had sprung to her feet.

'Monsieur Macon,' she exclaimed earnestly, 'is the chateau part of an estate? Would whoever owned the estate own the farms hereabouts?'

The proprietor looked taken aback now, and not altogether happy at her question. It was as though she had overstepped the mark of what was proper to ask, and he levered his over-indulged body up from his chair.

'It is possible, *mademoiselle*,' he agreed stiffly. 'Now if you will excuse me?'

Harriet clenched her fists. 'Just—just one more thing, *monsieur*,' she appealed. 'Who owns the chateau?'

The proprietor smoothed his apron. 'Why do you wish to know?' he asked evasively.

Harriet glanced down at Susan. 'I—we—as a matter of fact, I've bought a property only a few kilometres from here.' She hesitated. 'I was curious to know who used to own it, that's all. You see,' she hastened on, 'I bought it through an agent, in Paris.'

The proprietor looked suspicious now. 'But you said you needed somewhere to stay,' he reminded her.

Harriet managed to prevent the surge of heat that seemed to be moistening every inch of skin on her body from filling her face with revealing colour. 'Er—naturally the place needs airing,' she protested, but she could see the man was not entirely convinced. 'You were saying. . .?'

The proprietor frowned and looked doubtfully about him, as if hoping for another customer on whom to devote his attentions. But the tiny café was deserted at this hour of the day, and Harriet guessed he was wishing he had closed up earlier.

'At least tell me the name of the chateau,' she pressed him urgently, reasoning that whatever the chateau's name, the owner's would not be dissimilar.

'It is the Chateau de Rochefort, *mademoiselle*,' he told her reluctantly. 'Anyone could tell you that.'

'Thank you.' Harriet gathered up her handbag and the map she had carried with her, and together with Susan left the café.

'What was all that about?' exclaimed Susan, as soon as they were outside and out of earshot. 'What does it matter who owns the chateau?'

Harriet gave a secret smile. 'I should have thought it was obvious.'

'Well, it's not.'

Susan was getting irritable, and Harriet gave in. 'Don't you see? Monsieur Frond is an agent, acting on behalf of the owners. The house—our house—was probably owned by the Count de Rochefort, or whatever the owner of that chateau up there calls himself.'

'Oh, I see.' Susan's face cleared. 'You mean—perhaps we should speak to him, is that what you mean?'

'Something like that.'

'But when? Now?'

'Heavens, no.' Harriet shook her head, and consulted her watch. 'It's nearly six. There's no point in us trying to find our way there tonight and getting lost in the process. No, we'll have to leave that until tomorrow.'

'So what are we going to do?' exclaimed Susan.

Harriet gave her a rueful look. 'Well, I'm loath to say it, but I guess we go back.'

'To the house!' Susan sounded highly delighted.

'Yes,' agreed Harriet dryly, 'to the house. But

I suggest we buy a few things before we go. Like some cleaning materials, for example, and some disinfectant.'

The car was already loaded with food for a week, but Harriet added a carton of milk and some fresh eggs for good measure before bundling their recent acquisitions on to the back seat.

'I hope you realise this isn't going to be a picnic,' she warned Susan, when her niece seemed incapable of wiping the smile from her face, and Susan laughed.

'I don't believe you're really as sorry to be going back as you pretend,' she insisted, and although Harriet disputed this, she couldn't help the surge of pleasure she felt when the Fiat turned on to the bumpy, tree-lined lane. The setting sun through the trees was gilding the tiles of the house, casting a concealing mantle of shadow over the chipped and peeling walls so that like a courtesan at dusk, it did not reveal its flaws.

It was only as Harriet brought the car to a halt in front of the house that she saw the smoke emitting from the chimney, and her heart palpitated wildly as all the wild stories she had heard of ghosts and unearthly presences tumbled through her head.

'The chimney's smoking!' cried Susan in alarm. 'Harriet, we didn't light the fire!'

One look at the girl's haunted face was enough to bring Harriet to her senses. 'No, we didn't,' she agreed grimly, thrusting open the door and climbing out with a degree of composure that inwardly amazed her.

Even so, her legs felt uncomfortably shaky as she traversed the short weed-strewn path to the open door, and her heart leapt into her throat when a tall figure appeared in the entrance, his face shadowed by the sun on her eyes. She halted uncertainly, wondering if he was a tramp or a squatter, wondering whether he might be violent; and then he spoke, and her whole world dissolved around her.

'*Harriet*!' he said incredulously. '*Mon dieu*, Harriet, is it really you?'

CHAPTER TWO

HARRIET stood as if frozen to the spot. She was aware of Susan coming up the path to stand behind her, of her touching her arm and whispering: 'Who is it? Harriet, do you know him?' But she made no immediate reply. She was too stunned. Too shocked. Too lacking in control of her vocal cords to allow anything to escape them which might reveal to this man exactly what finding him here had done to her. Did she know him? Oh, God! she thought vehemently, if only she didn't. If only she had never met him! But that still didn't explain what he was doing here.

It helped to hold tightly on to her handbag, and as her eyes adjusted themselves to the light she was able to see him clearly. Without his instant recognition of her, she wondered if she would have recognised him; and then dismissed the thought as unworthy of her intelligence. Of course she would have recognised him. He had not changed so very much, except perhaps that he was thinner, and in consequence the lines of his face were more deeply drawn. There were more streaks of grey in his hair than she remembered, but why not? It had been eight years, after all, and he must be what? Forty—forty-one, now? Maybe even forty-two. Yet his hair was still predominantly dark, and presently overlapped the collar of the rough shirt he was wearing. He had obviously been cleaning out the grate, and his hands and forearms were blackened with soot; so he made no attempt to touch her, just looked at her with those dark, heavy-lidded eyes she remembered so well.

'Harriet,' he said again. 'I did not know it was you!'

'What was me?'

The words came out sharp and staccato, not at all like her usual husky tones, and his dark brows lifted interrogatively.

'I did not realise you were the purchaser of the house,' he explained simply. 'What did you think I meant?'

Harriet chose not to answer this, and glancing round nervously at Susan, made a feeble introduction: 'This is Monsieur Laroche, Susan. He—I—we met some years ago, in Paris. At—at an auction.'

This was such a travesty of the truth that Harriet was half afraid he might contradict her, but she ought to have guessed he would not commit himself so far.

'How do you do, Susan?' He inclined his head politely, displaying his dirt-grimed hands. 'I regret I am unable to offer a salutation. My apologies.'

Susan smiled a trifle uncertainly, looking to Harriet for guidance, and her aunt cleared her throat. 'You still haven't explained what you're doing here—*monsieur*,' she prompted abruptly, and suffered the full strength of his gaze upon her.

'Did I not? But then I would have thought it was obvious. I am afraid I have to offer apologies for the state of the house, but my excuse is that I did not learn until yesterday that Frond had in fact found a buyer.'

'You mean——' Harriet stared at him aghast. 'You mean, *you* were the previous owner?'

'That is correct.'

Harriet could hardly believe it. But then she could hardly believe any of this. Even Laroche himself was far removed from the sophisticated man she had met in the St Germain salerooms in Paris. The clothes he had worn then had been immaculate and expensive, fitting his lean body as only expert tailoring can. Now of course she had to make allowances for the fact that he had been cleaning out the grate, but nothing could alter the fact that the shirt he was wearing was made of rough homespun, and the tight-fitting jeans that moulded the powerful muscles of his legs were worn and shabby.

'You lived—here?' she echoed faintly, feeling a growing revulsion for the place if this were so, but he shook his head.

'No, I did not say that. I live—well, a few kilometres from here, but when I learned from Frond that the house had been sold, I realised he could have no conception as to the state it was in.'

Harriet heaved a sigh. 'I see.'

A sudden crackling from within made him turn his head swiftly, and excusing himself he went back to attend to the sticks which were burning brightly in the grate. Harriet exchanged a helpless look with Susan, and then followed him.

The room seemed smaller with his presence by the fireplace. But she noticed that the debris had been swept away, and some attempt at cleaning the table and wooden seats had been made.

'You did this?' she asked disbelievingly, and he nodded.

'I swept upstairs yesterday evening,' he explained, feeding more wood on to the flames, 'but I did not have time to attend to everything. As you can see, it is very primitive.' He paused, but when she made no comment, he straightened to stand facing them again. 'You may look around, of course, but if you feel the house is not what you were led to believe, I shall quite understand. Naturally, I cannot blame Frond, but I can instruct him to refund your payment immediately.'

Susan looked anxiously up at her aunt. Laroche's English was much better than Harriet's French, and there was no mistaking his meaning. Susan's feelings were unmistakable, too.

'As—as a matter of fact we were here earlier,' Harriet admitted reluctantly. 'We looked around then.'

'Ah.' He did not look surprised. 'I thought I had not locked the door.'

Harriet gasped. 'You have a key!'

His expression grew wry. 'But of course. I have just told you. I did not know Frond had sold the place.'

'Well, if we're staying here, naturally I shall expect you to surrender it,' stated Harriet stiffly, and his mouth revealed a decidedly cynical twist.

'Naturally,' he assured her mockingly, and she felt the betraying heat enveloping her neck. It made her aware of the low cleavage of her blouse, and of how dishevelled she must appear. Until then, she had been so absorbed with his appearance, she had paid little heed to her own.

Now her fingers went automatically to secure that revealing button, and as if aware of her discomfort, he turned away once more to check the fire. With the shadows of dusk darkening the lane outside, the fire was a cheerful sight, and like the setting sun earlier, its bright reflection gave the room an unexpected charm. With the beams swept clean of dust, and a fresh coat of emulsion on the walls, it might not look half bad, thought Harriet in a moment of weakness, but the house was no longer the deterrent; the man facing the hearth had taken its place.

Susan tugged at her sleeve. 'We are going to stay, aren't we?' she mouthed desperately, and Harriet made an impatient gesture. 'Please!'

Susan was determined, but Harriet refused to be blackmailed. All right, so it had been her idea

to bring her niece away for a couple of months
until all the trauma of her parents' death had
died down, but if *he*—she refused to think of
him by his Christian name—if *he* was prepared
to give her her money back, there was absolutely
no reason why she shouldn't buy another house,
or a cottage, in another part of the country
entirely. Yet she had always loved this area, and
she had wanted to stay.

But that was before she had known who her
neighbours might be. How could she stay here,
only a stone's throw from *him* and his family?
How could she bear to know that she might run
into him at any time—into him, or his wife!
Besides, he might view her presence here as an
open invitation to take up where he had left off,
and that he would never do. *Never!* Even so, his
presence here puzzled her, and she wondered
how long he had undertaken menial tasks
himself.

'There! That seems to be burning satisfactorily,' he observed at last, and moved to the
sink to rinse his filthy hands. 'Are you planning
to spend the night here?'

Harriet wrapped the strap of her handbag
round her wrist. 'We were,' she conceded
shortly. 'We—we did go into the village, looking for an inn, but a Monsieur—Macon—?'

'Macon, *oui*?'

'—he told us there were no inns hereabout.'

'No, that is true,' he nodded. 'Although
recently an American company have been trying

to buy the chateau to turn it into a luxury hotel.'

'The Chateau de Rochefort?' inquired Harriet involuntarily, and he frowned.

'You have been there?'

'Oh, no.' She shook her head. 'We just thought. . . It doesn't matter.' She gave Susan a thoughtful look, and then added: 'Perhaps we could let you know tomorrow whether—well, whether we intend to stay.' She consulted her watch. 'It's getting rather late, and we're hungry.'

He dried his hands on a handkerchief he pulled out of his jeans pocket. It was not new but it was spotlessly clean, and she found herself speculating exactly what his position was. His circumstances were intriguing, even if he deserved whatever kind of retribution this might be, she thought maliciously.

'How will you sleep?' he asked, thrusting his handkerchief away again. 'The bed upstairs is not fit to use.'

'I don't think that need concern you, Monsieur Laroche,' Harriet retorted coldly, and had the satisfaction of seeing a faint trace of colour darken the brown skin covering his cheekbones.

'I did not mean to pry,' he said quietly, and she felt reproved. But before she could make any further comment, he added: 'If you do decide to stay, I will supply you with two single beds to take the place of the one upstairs, which must be destroyed.'

Harriet did not thank him. After all, she

justified herself angrily, the house had been sold furnished, and no one could argue that a bed was an absolute necessity.

'Where's the cooker?' Susan asked suddenly, and Harriet glanced round impatiently.

'There is no cooker—at present,' Laroche told them. 'Some years ago, the oven beside the fire was the only facility, but the last tenants of the house were provided with a Calor gas stove. Unfortunately it was removed some months ago. I will see that it is restored also if you choose to stay.'

Harriet sighed. 'But how can we make a hot drink?' she protested, momentarily shaken out of her incommunicative state, and he indicated an iron kettle on the hearth.

'I regret you will have to boil water in that for this evening,' he said. 'Unless. . .' He paused, his eyes probing Harriet's. 'Unless you care to join my family and myself for supper?'

How dared he?

Harriet dragged her gaze away from his feeling a sick awareness in the pit of her stomach. How could he invite her to share his supper, to sit at the same table as his wife and family, in the full knowledge of their previous relationship?

Almost choking on the words, she refused his invitation, and he moved his shoulders in a way that betrayed his Gallic ancestry. 'As you wish,' he acceded equably, and moved towards the door. 'I will return in the morning for your decision.' He indicated the lamp hanging from the ceiling. 'There is oil inside. Can you light it?'

Harriet straightened her spine. 'I should think so, *monsieur*. Goodnight.'

'*Bonsoir*,' he responded politely, and with a brief smile at Susan, he left them, striding away down the path to the lane.

Harriet waited until he reached the lane, and then hastened to the window, hushing Susan when she tried to speak to her, and watching which direction he took. He turned away from the road which ran between Bel-sur-Baux and Rochelac, and instead, entered the copse of trees that ran down to the stream, confirming Harriet's speculation that one could walk to the village that way. She waited until he had disappeared from sight, and then sank back against the wall, one hand pressed quellingly to the nervous pulse throbbing in her throat.

Susan stared at her for several seconds, and then she asked impatiently: 'Who is he? What's going on?'

Harriet straightened, shaking her head. 'I've told *you*. He—I—we met several years ago in Paris.'

'Is he in the antique business, too?' exclaimed Susan in surprise.

'I don't know.'

'But you said you met him at an auction!'

'We did.' Harriet flapped her hand about dismissingly. 'Look, we haven't time to talk about it now. It will be dark soon, and we still have the car to unload.'

Susan regarded her sulkily. 'You can't brush it off, just like that. You didn't just meet him once, did you? I'm not a baby. I could tell there was more to it than that.'

'Oh, Susan. . .' Harriet walked out of the house.

'Well! What went wrong?' demanded Susan, following her. 'I mean, he's rather dishy, isn't he? He reminded me of Sacha Distel.'

'Oh, good lord, he's nothing like Sacha Distel!' said Harriet crossly. 'Are you going to help me carry these things in, or not?'

Susan shrugged, and lifted a box of groceries. 'Did you have an affair with him?' she asked casually, and for a moment her aunt was too stunned to speak. 'Well,' she went on, carrying the groceries into the house. 'People do, you know. I even know girls of my age who—'

'I'd prefer not to discuss the matter any further,' Harriet essayed, depositing their sleeping bags on the kitchen table. 'Now, do you want tea or coffee? It's all the same to me.'

'Well, at least tell me his name,' exclaimed Susan, looking at her appealingly, and Harriet sighed.

'Why?'

'I'd just like to know, that's all. I'll stop asking questions if you tell me, honestly.'

Harriet hesitated. 'Will you?'

'Yes. Yes, I promise.'

Harriet bent over the box of groceries. 'His name's André. André Laroche. Now, can we please get some work done?'

The kettle, after a scouring at the sink, boiled remarkably quickly, and cold ham and cheese, with some of the crusty bread from the *patisserie*, went down very well with hot coffee. With the lamp lighted, and the door closed against the encroaching darkness outside, it was all rather cosy, and Susan said so.'

'We haven't sampled the delights of washing in cold water yet, and remember, there's no bathroom,' Harriet observed ruthlessly. 'Did you see the privy when you went down to the stream?'

Susan nodded ruefully. 'It's just outside the back door, actually.'

'Chemical, of course?' Susan nodded, and Harriet grimaced. 'Oh, well, I can hardly blame anyone for that. I knew the conditions would not measure up to what we were used to, but—'

'We are going to stay, aren't we?' Susan broke in eagerly. 'It's not as bad as you expected, is it? And if André Laroche provides us with two single beds. . .'

'Monsieur Laroche to you,' Harriet corrected her sharply, and then went on brusquely: 'I don't know what I'm going to do, Susan. If—if Monsieur Laroche is prepared to give me my money back, I might be well advised to take it.'

'Oh, no!'

Susan was aghast, and Harriet spread her hands helplessly. 'We—I can buy another house,

Susan. Somewhere else. Somewhere—less—
isolated.'

'But I like it here!' declared Susan, pushing
her fringe out of her eyes, and Harriet caught
her lower lip between her teeth.

It was at times like these that her niece most
resembled her mother. Unlike Harriet, Sophie
had been red-haired, with the blue eyes her
daughter had inherited. Harriet's hair was much
fairer, although her skin was not, and she had
never had the problems with tanning that Sophie
had suffered. Harriet's eyes, too, were firmly
brown, and therefore stronger than Susan's
slightly myopic vision.

It was this weakening memory of her dead
sister that made Harriet hesitate now, when all
her instincts urged her to get rid of the house
while she could, and leave Rochelac before she
was forced into a situation she would regret.

'Susan. . . Susan. . .' she began persuasively,
but her niece had her father's strength of will.

Facing her aunt stubbornly, she said: 'You
promised me we would stay here. You said
you'd always wanted to spend time in the
Dordogne, exploring the castles and the caves!
Now you're changing your mind. And all
because of that man!'

'That's not true!' Harriet's cheeks were red
now. 'Susan, you know I had serious doubts
about this place the minute I saw it.'

'But you'd come back, hadn't you? You were

going to give it a chance. Until you met André Laroche!'

'Susan!'

'I don't believe you don't like the house. We could make it super, and you know it. What's wrong? Did he walk out on you or something? Is that why you're still an old maid at twenty-six!'

As soon as the words were uttered, Susan regretted them, and she threw her head down on her folded arms and began to sob as if her heart would break. Harriet let her cry for a while, realising there was more behind her tears than disappointment at her indecision. Susan was by no means recovered from the shock of both her parents being killed in a multiple pile-up on the M1 six weeks ago, and perhaps she was being unreasonable in imagining she could shunt the child about wherever the fancy took her. After all, she could have met André again any time, at any one of a dozen sales she had visited in France since. Perhaps it was a good idea to exorcise his ghost once and for all. Certainly the memory of that period of her life had cast a shadow over all subsequent relationships to the extent that Susan was not altogether unjustified in calling her an old maid. Only Charles got anywhere near her, and their association was governed by a mutual love of antiquities.

At last she got up and went across to the girl, sliding an arm about her shoulders. Susan uttered a muffled apology, and buried her face against her, sniffing and groping blindly for her handkerchief. But the storm was over, and presently she lifted her head and looked sheepishly up at her aunt.

'I'm sorry.'

'Don't be silly.' Harriet spoke cheerfully. 'I'm not offended. You could be right—about me being an old maid, I mean.'

'But you're not,' protested Susan vehemently. 'You're just devoted to your career, that's all. All my friends think you're terribly sophisticated, and your clothes are always so—elegant. You're not a bit like—Mummy, I mean—you've never shown any interest in getting married or having a family, have you? But I expect you've known heaps of men. . .'

'You make me sound like a selfish bitch!' remarked Harriet, her smile hiding the pain the child's words had unknowingly inflicted. If only Susan knew, she thought bitterly, if only she knew!

'Well, anyway, that's what I want, too,' Susan insisted loyally. 'I don't want to get married until I'm thirty, at least. I'm going to make a career for myself first.'

Harriet turned away to carry their empty cups to the sink. Outside it was completely dark now, and insects attracted by the light, were beginning to throw themselves against the murky glass of the window. She had Sellotaped pieces of cardboard over the broken panes, and now, watching some of the hairy-legged moths making their futile attacks, she was glad she had. She was no lover of insects in any form.

'Where are we going to sleep?' asked Susan, apparently prepared to leave the question of what Harriet intended to do until the morning, and her aunt frowned.

'In here, I think,' she decided thoughtfully. 'The air in the *salon* is definitely musty, and I'd like to be sure all the corners have been swept out before lying down in there.'

'All right.' Fully recovered now, Susan unrolled the sleeping bags, and spread them out before the fire. 'Can I miss having a wash tonight? I feel too sleepy.'

Harriet nodded her agreement. 'All right. Do you want to go outside first, or shall I?'

'I'll go,' Susan offered with a grin. 'I'll make sure there are no spiders lurking about. At least that's one thing I'm good for!'

An owl hooted as Harriet let herself back into the house a few minutes later, and she suppressed the hysterical laughter that welled up inside her. Why was it she had never anticipated what it might be like after dark? she wondered, securing the bolt with a definite feeling of relief.

For all she was tired, Harriet did not sleep well. She had too many things to think about, not least what she intended doing next day. Susan, lying curled up in her sleeping bag beside her, obviously had no such anxieties, and Harriet envied her her ability to leave her problems to solve themselves.

But where did that leave her? What could she

do, knowing how distressed Susan would be if she insisted on selling the house? And how long might it take to negotiate another sale even if her money was instantly forthcoming? Charles had only given her eight weeks' leave of absence, and besides, Susan had to return to school in September.

There seemed nothing for it but to remain where she was, however distasteful to her that might be. It was only eight weeks, and surely, once they were satisfactorily settled there would be no need for them to see André Laroche. It wasn't as if they had any rent to pay, and no doubt his wife would soon object if he started paying undue attention to the new owners. Was she so unsure of herself and her feelings that she must succumb to the absurd and cowardly notion to flee? The past was dead; the pain she was experiencing was the vulnerability of an old wound that had suddenly been scratched by a heavy and insensitive hand. And like all injuries, exposure to the air might effect the swiftest cure. But nothing could convince her that she would ever feel anything but hatred and contempt for the man who had awakened her so rudely to the cruel facts of life.

CHAPTER THREE

HARRIET was awakened by the sound of Susan running water into the iron kettle. Somehow, she had managed to rake over the embers of the fire without disturbing her aunt, and with the aid of some dry twigs and the torn-up cardboard boxes in which they had carried their crockery and groceries, she had succeeded in rekindling the fire to boil some water for breakfast.

Harriet stirred sleepily, aware that apart from a certain stiffness in her spine, she felt reasonably refreshed. Outside, the birds had already set up a morning chorus, and the smell of blossom from the garden was scenting the air with its fragrance. Everything seemed less sombre with the sun filtering in through the grubby panes, although its brilliance again illuminated the rooms' shortcomings.

She had not undressed, and now she wriggled out of her sleeping bag feeling distinctly hot and sticky, reflecting ruefully that Susan's description of her the night before was now far from accurate.

'You sleep well,' her niece remarked cheerfully, setting the kettle squarely on the flames, and Harriet refrained from revealing that it had

37

been well into the early hours before she had closed her eyes.

'Did you?' she asked instead, getting to her feet and wrapping up the sleeping bag, and Susan nodded vigorously.

'Like a log,' she exclaimed. 'It must be the air. Hmm!' She took a deep breath at the open doorway. 'Isn't it divine?'

Harriet tied the sleeping bag into its roll and set it on the table. 'That stream,' she ventured thoughtfully, 'do you think it's very shallow?'

'Our stream?' Susan was eager. 'I shouldn't think it's very deep, if that's what you mean.'

Harriet grimaced. 'Could I wash there, do you think? I feel awfully grimy, and I want a thorough wash before I change my clothes.'

Susan shrugged. 'I'll go and see, if you like.'

'No.' Harriet shook her head. 'No, don't bother. I'll go myself. Did we unpack any towels last night?'

Armed with soap and towel, toothbrush and paste, Harriet opened the door which led into the tangled garden at the back of the house. Like the front, it was overgrown with shrubs and weeds, but as she trampled her way towards the sound of the water as it tumbled over its rocky course, she saw the remains of what had once been a herb garden, and smelled the delicious fragrance of mint and rosemary.

The stream was clear and fast-running, and Harriet felt almost inclined to taste it, but she decided not to take any chances. Instead, she took off her sandals and dipped her feet into its chilly shallows, smiling as the coldness tickled her toes. Downstream a short way, a cleft in the rock formed a small pool, and Harriet thought longingly of submerging her sticky body. Washing was all very well, but there was nothing to compare with taking a bath, and after assuring herself that she was completely alone, she stripped off her shirt and pants, and plunged bodily into the water. Sitting on the sandy bottom, the water lapped coolly about her breasts, and she soaped herself luxuriously, enjoying herself as she had not done since she was a child. In her apartment in London, she had a large modern bathroom, with a step-in bath and shining chrome-plated shower, and she had forgotten what it was like to enjoy the simple things of life. Her parents' home in Surrey was the same, with every kind of labour-saving device, from washing machines to central heating. But sitting here she couldn't help wondering whether they were not losing more than they gained.

A brisk rub down with the towel restored the glow of warmth to her skin, and she pulled on her pants and shirt again to run back to the house. She didn't bother fastening them, she intended changing as soon as she got back, and she came into the house eagerly, intending to tell Susan what she had done.

The sight of André Laroche lounging by the sink, talking to Susan as she buttered the toasted remains of the loaf they had bought the previous afternoon, brought her up short, and she was glad of the wet towel to hide her embarrassment. She wondered uneasily which way he had come, and whether he had seen her in the stream. Would she have heard a footfall over the musical sounds of the water? The idea of his eyes observing her impromptu ablutions did not bear thinking about.

'Good morning.' He straightened, his greeting instinctively polite, but she sensed his probing regard and pressed the towel closer.

Harriet wondered if she was imagining the irony in his tones. 'You're early, *monsieur*,' she countered, ignoring his remark, 'it's barely eight o'clock!'

'Some of us have work to do,' he replied smoothly. 'Had you not been up, I should have had to come back later.'

'Would you like some coffee, Monsieur Laroche?'

Susan's words successfully forestalled any response her aunt was about to make, and Harriet took the opportunity to disappear into the small *salon* where they had left their suitcases. It took only a few moments to find a clean shirt and striped cotton pants, and she pushed her feet into her wedged sandals, glad of the extra height they provided. Although she was a tall girl, André could still top her by a few inches, but if she could decrease the disparity so much the better.

When she came back into the kitchen, her

straight hair brushed and shining, she felt more able to deal with him, although she still felt slightly disarmed without any make-up. Susan had made the coffee and was presently pouring their visitor a cup, and Harriet waited impatiently for him to ask the question which must be foremost in his mind. But he didn't. He acknowledged Harriet's return with a casual quirk of his eyebrow, and then complimented Susan on her housewifely talents. The girl beamed beneath his deliberate flattery, and Harriet felt her teeth clenching so tightly together she was amazed they didn't snap.

Susan handed her aunt some coffee, but Harriet declined the hastily proffered toast, refusing to answer the appeal in her niece's eyes. In spite of all her practical reasoning of the night before, she was desperately tempted to tell him they were leaving.

'Your niece has been telling me you are an expert on ceramics,' he remarked suddenly, and Harriet flashed Susan an irate glance.

'You know how children exaggerate,' she retorted shortly, and ignoring Susan's indignation, added: 'I imagine you'd like to know what I've decided to do about the house.'

André put down his cup on the table. This morning he was wearing black denim jeans that hung on his hips and an olive green shirt that gave his dark-skinned features a sallow cast. As he turned slowly to face her, she conceived the absurd notion that he had been putting off asking for her decision, and the thought caused a momentary sapping of her will. Dear God, she thought weakly, he couldn't want her to stay, could he?

'You are leaving?'

It was more of a statement than a question, and Harriet was briefly diverted by Susan's involuntary gasp of protest. Then she raised her eyes to his, and distractedly found herself refuting the charge.

'I don't have enough time to find another house and negotiate another sale,' she defended herself tersely. 'But naturally I expect you to provide the two beds you promised, and a cooking stove of some kind.'

'*Naturellement*!' It was perhaps a sign of his distraction that he spoke in his own language, and Harriet was forced to look away from the frank inquiry of his gaze. She was half angry with herself for agreeing to stay, and the inclination to blame him for this impossible situation was almost overwhelming. It was useless telling herself that he had been an innocent party to the affair. Childishly, she wanted a scapegoat, and who better than André Laroche?

Footsteps on the path outside provided an unexpected diversion, and Harriet looked up in surprise as a boy of perhaps fifteen or sixteen appeared in the open doorway. He was an attractive boy, tall for his age with shoulder-length dark hair and lean intelligent features. He paused in the aperture, his hands raised to support him-

self against the frame at either side, and his eyes
flickered interestedly over the occupants of the
room. Then he saw the man, and a grin spread
over his face.

'*Te voilà*!' he exclaimed, with satisfaction. '*Je
t'ai cherché partout*!'

Harriet knew at once who he was. The simi-
larity was unmistakable, and besides, he had
inherited his father's eyes. He was completely
unselfconscious standing there, curiosity
deepening his regard.

André flexed his shoulder muscles rather
impatiently, she felt, before looking at the boy
without apparent affection. 'This house no
longer belongs to us, Paul,' he declared curtly,
in English. 'And Louise could have told you
where I was.'

Louise! Unwillingly Harriet was aware that
she was holding her breath. Was Louise his
wife's name? Would he use his mother's name
to the boy?

'*Comment donc*!'

Paul met the man's eyes defiantly, and for a
few seconds a silent battle of wills ensued. Then
he looked away again, his attention passing over
Susan's flushed features to rest of Harriet's with-
drawn countenance.

'*Pardonnez-moi, mesdemoiselles*!' he apolo-
gised, without conviction, and she heard the
sound of André's angrily expelled breath.

'This is my son—Paul,' he stated, rather
unnecessarily Harriet felt, but she chose to

acknowledge the introduction, if only to
thwart him.

'*Bonjour*, Paul,' she offered smoothly, and the
boy surveyed her with added interest.

'You must be Miss Ingram,' he remarked
slowly, and she was impressed by his effortless
transition from French to English. 'My father
told us you had bought this place unseen.' He
stepped aside, ignoring André's evident dis-
approval. 'Have you decided to stay at
Rochefort?'

'*Rochefort*?' Harriet frowned, recognising the
name of the chateau. 'Don't you mean—
Rochelac?'

Paul glanced mockingly at his father, and then
shrugged his shoulders. 'Probably,' he affirmed
indifferently. 'Are you going to stay?'

'That is not your concern,' put in his father
grimly, but Paul was not deterred.

'I might be able to be of some assistance,' he
protested innocently, but Harriet could see his
father was not deceived. Perhaps she ought not
to be either, she thought shrewdly, and turning
to André said:

'Don't let us keep you, *monsieur*. As you said,
you have work to do.'

'Very well.' André cast his son another irritated look. 'I will have the other items of
furniture delivered later this morning.'

'Thank you.'

Harriet's lips moved in the polite semblance
of a smile, but there was no warmth in it. Paul

glanced from one to the other of them, and his eyes narrowed speculatively, but his father's hand upon his shoulder propelled him towards the door.

'If you have any other problems, don't hesitate to get in touch with me,' André added as they left, but it was not until they had gone that Harriet realised she did not even know where he lived.

As soon as they were alone, Susan rushed across the the room and hugged her aunt. 'Thank you, thank you!' she cried excitedly, but Harriet was in no mood to appreciate her gratitude.

'Don't thank me,' she averred shortly. 'We're both going to have to work like slaves before we can begin to enjoy this holiday!'

At least hard labour served to put all thoughts of André Laroche out of her mind. With the aid of a wedge of wood and a hammer, she managed to get the upstairs window open, although shutting it again might prove a problem, and set Susan to scrubbing the bedroom floor. Meanwhile, she shifted everything out of the kitchen and set about cleaning the walls and cupboards. The *salon* would have to wait, but as they would not be spending much time in there, it wasn't so important.

Outside, she discovered a shed adjoining the privy which contained some primitive gardening tools. Picking up a heavy scythe, she swung it experimentally through the air, and got quite a shock when a cluster of sunflower heads fell at her feet. It was sharper than she had imagined, and surveying the tangled garden she thought that perhaps it was just as well. But like the *salon* the garden would have to wait until another day.

Back in the kitchen, the air was stifling. Susan's fire was still smouldering away, but Harriet was loath to put it out until the cooking stove arrived. They had not had a hot meal since yesterday lunchtime, and she was determined to fry some eggs and bacon today, on the fire if necessary. She was not keen to put her sleek, non-stick frying pan over the flames, but needs must, and Susan deserved something more substantial than bread and cheese.

By half past eleven, the kitchen was beginning to look presentable, although she needed some paint to colourwash the walls and ceiling. But at least it was clean, the table scrubbed and shining.

Upstairs, Susan had made a fair job of the bedroom, and together they tugged the old mattress downstairs and out into the garden. The frame took a little more dismantling, and they left the base for whoever brought the single beds to dispose of.

The sound of a lumbering vehicle making its way down the lane brought them both to the windows, and Harriet was relieved when she saw that it was a lorry loaded with furniture. Already the place was beginning to assume their identity, and had it not been for André, she thought she would have been content.

The driver of the vehicle introduced himself as Bertrand Madoc. He was a short, thick-set individual, with a shock of grey hair and twinkling button brown eyes. Harriet thought he was scarcely big enough to carry the bed-frame down from upstairs, but she was soon proved wrong. He was immensely strong, and made light work of shifting out the base and the old washstand.

'I say,' exclaimed Susan in dismay, 'I've just cleaned that!' but Bertrand just shook his head.

'*Attendez, mademoiselle*!' he told her reassuringly, and Susan unwillingly agreed to wait and see.

It soon became apparent that two single beds and a cooking stove were not all André had despatched. There was a small *armoire* and dressing table, beautifully carved, that Harriet recognised as being old and rather valuable; a pair of matching velvet chairs and a chaise-longue, somewhat faded, but obviously period pieces, and a nineteenth-century *escritoire* which when the dresser was removed did not look out of place in the small *salon*.

Bertrand would have carried the dresser out to the lorry, but Harriet stopped him, realising that it was exactly what she needed in the kitchen to store plates and dishes. She just wished she had had time to clean out the *salon* before the new pieces were installed, but it was too late now.

It was irritating having to feel gratitude towards André, but his kindness could not be

denied. She wondered uncharitably whether this
was his way of putting her in his debt, and then
dismissed the notion by assuring herself that she
had paid him adequately for the privilege of
living here. Still, she couldn't help wondering
where he had got all these things from. Surely
it would have been cheaper to buy new modern
furniture than these period pieces, unless he had
access to some mouldering chateau. Not for the
first time she wondered what he had been doing
at the St Germain salerooms that day eight years
ago, and suddenly she realised why the name
Rochelac had seemed so familiar. Among the
articles for sale that day had been pieces from
the Chateau de Rochefort! Of course! Why
hadn't she remembered this before? So what was
André? Some sort of agent for the impoverished
aristocracy?

Bertrand completed his task in less than an
hour, refusing to accept Harriet's offer of
refreshment. Instead, he climbed back into his
lorry, and she had to hurry to catch him before
he closed the door of his cab. 'Please,' she
exclaimed in his language, 'thank—thank
Monsieur Laroche for me.'

'You will no doubt be able to thank him per-
sonally,' Bertrand replied comfortably, and with
a deprecating smile, reversed away.

Harriet walked back to the house speculating
on his words. He sounded so sure about it. Did
everyone know of André's visits to the house?
Did no one object? Well, she decided grimly,

she did, and displayed an unsmiling acceptance in the face of Susan's enthusiasm.

Still, she could not remain indifferent for long. The cooker, heated by Calor gas, was new and a gleaming oven invited-experimentation. The dresser, too, looked infinitely more attractive with plates on its shelves, and not even the gaps in the now-clean windows could detract the sun's rays from shining through the panes that were there.

Harriet carried their cases upstairs, and Susan unpacked their clothes while she made up the beds. Although the headboards were of reproduction design, the bases were interior sprung, and with the sprigged cotton bedspreads Harriet had brought gave the room a bright appearance.

Susan soon disposed of the suitcases. Trousers, skirts and dresses hung away easily in the *armoire*, while their underclothes folded neatly into the drawers of the dressing table.

'Oh, doesn't it look nice!' she exclaimed, when she had finished, the suitcases stowed away in a corner out of sight. 'Surely you're glad you stayed now, aren't you?'

Harriet relented, putting an arm around the girl's shoulders. 'All right,' she agreed. 'You were right—this place does have possibilities.'

But after lunch it was too hot to do anything else. Susan put on her bikini and took a dip in the stream, and then stretched out on a rug, impervious to Harriet's admonitions to watch out for ants.

Harriet herself carried the wooden rocker out-doors, and with the aid of a notebook and pencil, jotted down the items she thought they might need. But even that became too much of an effort after a while, and she allowed the pencil to fall from her hand and stretched out lazily. Not even a breeze stirred the trees in the lane, and the silence was broken only by the occasional sounds of birds and insects, and the soft babbling of the stream.

Unfortunately, with time on her hands, her thoughts turned irresistibly to André Laroche, and the amazing coincidence of his owning this house. Perhaps it was as well she had not probed more deeply into its history or she might never have come here at all.

Unwillingly, her mind drifted back to her first encounter with the man who was to have such a destructive influence on her life. Eight years ago, she had been eighteen and on her first buy-ing trip with Charles Hockney in Paris. She had been thrilled at the experience of handling items which hitherto she had only read about, and their visits to the various salerooms had revealed a wealth of beauty and craftsmanship even to her uneducated eyes. Perhaps that was when she had first conceived her love of porcelain—when she held a pair of exquisite Mennecy figures in her hands, and learned to distinguish the marks of the Duc de Villeroy, the factory's founder—or was it simply that afterwards she remembered every detail of that trip with an exactitude that far outweighed its importance?

Whatever the truth might be, she could still recall standing beside Charles at the back of the saleroom in the Place St Germain, watching the auctioneer at work. She had suddenly become aware that someone was watching her, and although Charles thought she was engrossed in the sale, she had turned her head and met the intent gaze of a man standing at the other side of the room. He was taller than many of the people there, lean and dark, with the kind of uneven features that are so much more attractive than bland good looks. Deep-set eyes, high cheekbones, a prominent nose, and a mouth that had a slightly cruel twist, she thought. She even remembered what he was wearing—a dark blue velvet suit and a matching silk shirt which on anyone else would have looked effeminate. Harriet had never encountered anyone like him before, and the way he was looking at her made her feel curiously weak inside, and just a little frightened. He wasn't like the young men she was used to associating with, and he certainly wasn't like Charles, who was plump and short-sighted, and inclined to baldness. She guessed this man was in his thirties, twenty years younger than Charles, with all the experience of a man who knows he is attractive to women.

Blind panic invaded her later when he made an excuse to speak to Charles—and through him to Harriet. But the panic had been unwarranted, she acknowledged now. He had been charming, *fascinating*, and so easy to talk to. He had asked her about her job and her ambitions, and how long she was staying in Paris, so that Harriet began to feel she really must be something special. She had left the saleroom in a state of euphoria which had only lasted as long as it took Charles to bring her down to earth again.

Then the following day he had telephoned her at the hotel, and she forgot Charles' warnings and agreed to meet him for dinner that evening. Charles did not approve, but he could not forbid her to go, and even if he had, she thought she would probably have disobeyed him.

André took her to a restaurant in Montmartre, where they ate grilled lobster and Camembert, and Harriet drank more wine than she had ever done before. It crossed her mind that he might be trying to get her slightly drunk, but by then she was too bemused to do anything about it.

But she need not have worried. André took her straight back to her hotel afterwards, and she was ashamed to admit that she was disappointed when he merely raised her fingers to his lips to say goodnight.

Charles, of course, was horrified when he discovered she had been drinking. 'A man like that must know what strong wine does to a girl of your age!' he declared. 'Have you no sense? What do you think your parents would say if they knew how you were carrying on?'

'I am eighteen, Mr Hockney,' Harriet replied. She and Charles were not on Christian name terms in those days, and the appellation served as a barrier to further protests. 'And my parents have never interfered in choosing my friends.'

She refrained from admitting that up to the present her boy-friends had all been known to her family, either through their parents or her two older sisters. But on the other hand, she had never known the excitement she felt in André's presence, and she was foolish enough to imagine she had everything under control.

However, it seemed that Charles' fears had been unfounded, for after that evening she did not see André again for several weeks. She and Charles returned to London, and in spite of a slightly hollow feeling every time she thought of Paris, she managed to get on with her life.

In those days, she was living at her parents' home in Guildford and travelling in to London every day. It meant a rush in the mornings and usually something of a scrum in the evenings, but her mother preferred it that way and Harriet had no objections. Apart from the people she met in the course of her work, all her friends lived in Guildford, and she would have missed the dances and parties attended by the group she went around with.

She was alone in the shop one afternoon when André walked in. She had given up hope of ever seeing him again by this time, almost convinced that what Charles had said was right: that he had merely been playing with her, and she had been fortunate to escape without injury. His unexpected appearance threw her into confusion, although he seemed different somehow—thinner perhaps and older—his greeting holding little of the usual charm she knew he could so effortlessly exhibit. Only his eyes remained the same, and they still told her they found her good to look at.

'What are you doing in London?' she asked, unable to think of anything more original to say, but he walked past her into the room at the back of the shop, and she had perforce to follow him.

Charles did not live over the shop. He had a very comfortable apartment in St John's Wood, but this room was used to entertain clients, and when Harriet reached the doorway, she saw that André was helping himself to a glass of Madeira.

'Your employer is out,' he remarked, studying the wine with frowning intensity. 'I watched him leave.' Then he looked up. 'Tell me, did you want to see me again?'

When Charles came back, the door was locked and the blinds were drawn, and he had to rattle long and noisily at the latch before Harriet came to let him in. He knew at once what he had interrupted, and Harriet was always amazed he didn't fire her on the spot. Instead, he and André had another glass of Madeira, while Harriet tried desperately to get things into perspective. She didn't know how André could calmly drink Charles' wine when only minutes before they had been lying together on the horsehair sofa where he was presently sitting; and then she saw the tremor of his wrist as he raised his glass to his lips and realised he was by no means as relaxed as he appeared.

Her own behaviour had appalled her. She would never have believed she could act so wantonly or feel so little remorse. From the moment André took her into his arms, she had been swamped with sensual feeling, unable to withstand the eager demands of her own body. She had never behaved that way with any man before—had never felt more than a fleeting curiosity about the intimate relationship between a man and a woman—and yet, being ruthlessly frank with herself, she knew that if Charles had not returned when he did, she would have submitted to anything André asked of her.

It was a little disturbing, like finding another person inside one's own skin, and she hoped she was not one of those awful women she had read about who succumbed to any man's ardour.

Yet, with hindsight, Harriet realised that life might have been simpler for her if she had been a woman like that. In the years following André's betrayal, she had yearned to feel emotion for some other man. But her emotions had been frozen, and the frigid reputation she had acquired had not been misplaced.

But at that time, her greatest fear had been that she might not see André again. This could not be a normal situation for him, having Charles behave as her father might have done. No doubt, the women he was used to associating with were casually experienced in such matters, and there would be no need for furtive embraces in the back room of a dusty antique shop. She imagined candlelit apartments and leopardskin rugs—or silken bodies between silken sheets. She gave no thought at all to the charms of her Scandinavian fair beauty, or the bloom of youth that no skilfully applied cosmetics could reproduce.

Her fear proved groundless. During the next three months, André spent a great deal of time in London, often flying in on Saturday morning and returning on Sunday evening. Charles approved no more now than he had done before, but he was wise enough to realise he could not influence her where André Laroche was concerned.

Harriet's parents were less understanding. They met André on several occasions, but her mother was of the opinion that he was too old for her, and her father was by no means satisfied by his casual references to his home in the Midi. Mr Ingram wanted to know about his family, and how he earned his living, and inevitably Harriet became suspicious with André's evasions.

Her relationship with him was not a satisfactory one. They were never alone together, always having to meet in public places. In truth, Harriet was relieved about this even while her senses cried out for a more intimate association. She could no longer trust herself where he was concerned, and her upbringing had been such that she felt hopelessly bound by the moralities of her parents. But that didn't stop her from thinking and dreaming, and reliving those moments in Charles' office, and wishing that Charles had not interrupted them when he had. . ..

The affair of André's parents brought matters to a head. For weeks, Harriet's mother had been complaining that although André had met her parents, she had not been invited to meet his. Didn't Harriet want to meet his family? Didn't she think she should?

Harriet, increasingly irritable and frustrated, told André what her mother had said. She gave him the news sulkily, making no attempt to mince her words, and didn't believe him when he told her that his parents were dead.

'Who do you live with, then?' she demanded suspiciously, but he refused to discuss it.

'What does it matter?' he asked gently. 'You and I are the only people who are concerned in this.'

Harriet would not leave it there, however. 'You've met my family,' she retorted, but his next words were not reassuring.

'You wanted me to meet your family,' he declared quietly. 'I did not look for the introduction.'

'You mean you didn't want to meet them?' Harriet exclaimed, and his casual shrug infuriated her. In a few moments she was quarrelling violently, allowing all the pent-up feelings of the past weeks to carry her on a wave of bitterness and self-pity. She hardly noticed that he took no part in the proceedings until he got up and left her sitting alone in the airport buffet.

The following days were the most painful Harriet had spent until that time. She went to and from work like an automaton, and apart from telling her mother that she and André were through, she made no reference to why. If her parents guessed they were tactful enough not to probe, but Harriet wondered if she would ever forgive them for what they had done.

Then, two weeks later, André telephoned. He rang her at the shop at a time when he knew Charles would be out for lunch, and the sound of his voice made her legs go weak at the knees.

'Have you forgiven me?' he asked, and at that moment she would have forgiven him anything.

'Have you forgiven me?' she countered, a revealing tremor in her voice.

There was silence for a moment, and then he said, almost angrily: 'I just wanted to apologise, Harriet. I just wanted to hear your voice one more time. Believe me, you have nothing to reproach yourself for.'

Panic filled her at that moment. 'What do you mean?' she cried. 'When am I going to see you?'

'You're not,' he replied flatly. 'I shan't be coming to London again.'

'But, André—' Her hand holding the receiver was slippery with perspiration. 'André, I want to see you again.'

'It's no use,' he told her harshly. 'Your

parents are right. You need someone younger—
someone like them. Someone who lives by their
kind of ideals.'

To her subsequent shame, Harriet lost her
head. 'I don't care about them!' she protested.
'I don't care about their ideals—' but hearing
the sob in her voice he interrupted her.

'You say that,' he muttered savagely, 'but you
don't mean it. *Le Bon Dieu* knows that I cannot
go on seeing you without—' he broke off
abruptly and she was terrified he was going to
hang up on her.

'Let me come and see you,' she begged. 'Let
me come to Paris. I can tell them I'm going with
Mr Hockney. Please, André, don't say no!'

It was not easy to persuade him, although with
the cynicism of experience, Harriet wondered
whether he had not known exactly how to bait
his hook. She had gone to Paris—and spent the
weekend with him at an hotel in the Rue de
Rivoli.

In spite of everything that came after, that still
remained the most exciting weekend of her life.
Paris seemed like the most romantic city in the
world, and she was eighteen and in love, and
with the one man above all others who could
make her forget everything she used to hold
most dear.

It had been a natural progression that they
should spend their nights together. From the
moment he met her at the airport, she was in his
arms, and here it was accepted that André should

stop in the street and seek her mouth with his own. Harriet just wanted to be with him, day and night, and the torment of their weeks of separation swept away the inhibitions which had kept them apart.

Returning to London was the worst part. She had half expected that André would ask her to stay, or at the least come with her, but he didn't. He came to the airport, and waved as her plane taxied along the runway, and that was the last she saw of him.

She did get a letter, though, a letter which she burned as soon as she had read it. Soon afterwards, she rented an apartment in town, and although things happened which reunited her with her parents, she never forgave herself for treating them so shabbily.

Charles was the only one who ever really understood what she had gone through. He was instrumental in finding her somewhere to live, and she had repaid him by working hard and taking much of the burden of the business from his shoulders. They were more like partners now than employer and employee, and when Harriet's eldest sister and her husband had been killed, it had been his suggestion that she should take her niece away for a while. She needed a holiday, he said, and that was true. Apart from weekends and bank holidays, she had not had any time off since Christmas, and she was beginning to feel the strain. But how much of a rest would she have here, she wondered, with the knowledge of André Laroche's presence colouring her every move? What would Charles say if he knew? What would her parents say?

Now she got up from her chair and wandered restlessly to the gate which led into the lane. She tugged out a long blade of grass, chewing on it absently as she stared towards the trees that hid the stream from view. If she followed the path that André had taken would she eventually come to his house? What would his wife say if she arrived uninvited? And his family? She wondered how many children he had. It would serve him right if she went along—and introduced herself, she thought angrily. She could imagine his consternation if he returned to find her with his wife, unable to be certain of how much she had revealed!

She pressed her lips together impatiently. Oh, God, was she going to spend the whole of her time here brooding over the past? It was dead! How many more times must she remind herself of that?

But as she walked back to the house, the insidious thought intruded that when she and André had spent that weekend together in Paris, Paul had been a little boy of only seven or eight years old.

CHAPTER FOUR

DURING the next few days, Harriet found she had plenty to do to fill her time. The following morning she drove into Rochelac, and as well as essential supplies like bread and milk, and meat and eggs, she bought paints and brushes, and some curtain material to replace the cardboard which had had to suffice up to the present. The only room that possessed curtains was the *salon*, but they were faded and threadbare, and besides, the new furniture deserved something better. It was going to be quite a task, sewing them all by hand, but Susan could help while she colourwashed the walls.

Although she had expected André would return to accept her thanks for the furniture, he did not, and contrarily, she was annoyed. She just wanted him to come and be done with it, she told herself irritably, and not leave them waiting indefinitely for his appearance. And yet wasn't that more in keeping with what she knew of him? she chafed, frustratedly dabbing a splash of honey-coloured paint from the front of her blue and white spotted top.

By the end of the week, the house was beginning to look good. Whitewashed walls in the kitchen were relieved by several cheap prints

Harriet had found on a stall on market day in Rochelac, and the dresser looked better with a coat of yellow paint. A couple of wool rugs added warmth to the stone floor, and the lamp which hung from the newly painted ceiling had been polished to a becoming shine.

It was the same in the *salon*, and upstairs in the bedroom, although Harriet had given up trying to get the window to close again. The loft was the only part of the house left uninvestigated. Harriet put off disturbing its cobwebby hollows, and even Susan's promise that she could deal with any unwelcome invaders did not change her mind.

With the house in order, Susan was all for exploring further afield. They had given Beynac-et-Cazenac only the most cursory of examinations, and the surrounding countryside was liberally scattered with castles and chateaux. From the commanding ramparts of Beynac Castle it was possible to see the whole of the Dordogne valley, and Harriet planned to visit Castelnaud which faced Beynac across the river. During the Hundred Years War, Castelnaud had been occupied by the English, and there had been many bloody skirmishes between the two opposing armies. It was an area deeply ingrained with history, not least the caves and grottoes where skeletons and paintings of prehistoric man had been found.

'Perhaps we ought to visit our local chateau first,' Susan suggested thoughtfully as she washed the breakfast dishes. 'I mean, if an American hotel group was trying to buy it as Monsieur Laroche said, it must have something, mustn't it?'

'I suspect it's the site they're interested in,' replied Harriet, noticing with some satisfaction that her legs were beginning to tan. 'These old landowners knew what they were doing, you know. They always built their chateaux or castles in positions of advantage, both for fortification and to command the best view. I suppose that's a fortification in itself—being able to see far enough afield to be forearmed against any attack.'

'Well, I'd like to see it anyway,' Susan insisted, and her aunt shrugged.

'There's no reason why we shouldn't. Actually, I was going to suggest going to Cahors, but that can wait until another day.'

Susan wiped her hands. 'You don't mind?'

'Why should I?' Harriet smiled. 'Besides, I think it's going to be too hot to go far, and Rochefort shouldn't be further than a few kilometres beyond Rochelac.'

The Fiat was already hot after standing in the sun for a couple of hours, and Harriet wound all the windows down before climbing behind the wheel. Brief shorts made her legs seem longer, and an orange sleeveless top drew attention to the honey-tinted skin of her arms. Susan beside her, dressed similarly in tee-shirt and shorts, grimaced at her own barely perceptible curves.

'Will I ever have a figure like yours?' she exclaimed, tugging impatiently at the hem of her shirt. 'And I wish my hair wasn't this colour. I wish it was blonde, like yours.'

'Redheads are far more distinctive,' Harriet reassured her with a smile. 'And of course you'll grow. We all do. Just remember, it's better to be too slim than too fat.'

Susan wrinkled her nose. 'Some girls at school have good figures. Jennifer Lewis wears a size thirty-six bra.'

Harriet started the car. 'Is she tall?'

'Only about my height—about five feet one or two.'

'And what's her hip measurement?'

'I don't know. About the same, I suppose.'

'Well, at fourteen, that's not an advantage.'

'All the boys are attracted to her,' Susan declared, with a sigh. 'They call me *Bones*!'

Harriet hid her amusement. 'I shouldn't let it worry you, love. Chunky ladies went out with padded shoulders. You'll make out, you'll see.'

Susan pursed her lips. 'That boy. . . Paul. . .' She paused to let the name register. 'He didn't notice me, did he? He was too busy looking at you. Do you think he's attracted to you?'

'Oh, good heavens!' Harriet narrowly avoided running into a horse-drawn wagon loaded with hay, which suddenly appeared round a bend in the road. Her exclamation was involuntary, and hid any reaction she might have made to Susan's question. Regaining her composure, she added carelessly: 'He was only showing off, Sue.'

'He liked you, though,' Susan insisted. 'I could see that. And why not?' she added gloomily. 'You attract men like honey attracts bees!'

Harriet gasped. 'Now come on, Susan! You're too young to make that kind of statement. Heavens! You sound exactly like—'

She broke off awkwardly, realising with impatience at her own thoughtlessness what she had been about to say, but Susan was not deceived.

'Mummy said it, actually,' she murmured huskily. 'One day when I asked her why you hadn't got married. She said—she said you weren't the type to be content with—with just one man.'

Harriet winced. 'I see.'

'You're not—cross, are you?'

Susan stared at her anxiously, and Harriet managed to give her a brief smile. 'Of course not,' she denied, swinging the car round a particular tortuous bend in the road, although it hurt to know that her sister had seen the number of her admirers as an example of her instability, not theirs.

Harriet had expected to have to drive through Rochelac to reach the chateau, but on the outskirts of the village there was a dusty signpost which indicated that the way to the chateau led down a tree-shadowed track that was scarcely wide enough to take the car. Harriet stopped uncertainly and looked all round them. Then she said:

'We're going to block the lane if we drive down there. And goodness knows what I'd do if I encountered another vehicle.'

'Let's walk,' suggested Susan at once, thrusting open her door. 'It can't be far, surely.'

Harriet got out of the car, too, and looked up doubtfully at the blue arc of the sky. The sun was gaining altitude, and very soon it would be completely overhead.

'I don't know,' she hesitated. 'Perhaps if we drive into the village, there'll be a proper road.'

'Oh, let's go this way!' begged Susan eagerly. 'If we don't get there in half an hour we can always come back.'

Harriet gave in. 'All right. But I'll have to park off the road. The shadow of those trees should keep it from getting too hot.'

The lane only led downwards for a short distance before turning up a steep incline that presently came out above the narrow course of a stream. The bank was thickly wooded, overgrown with flowering shrubs and creepers, and redolent with the scent of herbs. Below the stream had widened, tumbling rapids that cascaded swiftly over stones made slippery by ferns.

Harriet looked down at it frowningly for a moment, and then she exclaimed: 'That's our stream, I'm sure it is. Look!' She pointed some distance further downstream. 'Isn't that our house?'

Susan gasped. 'Gosh, so it is. This must be a short cut to the village.'

Harriet nodded her agreement. 'I wondered about that.'

Continuing along, they eventually came to a footbridge over the stream. The lane petered out at this point, and Harriet guessed the chateau was at the head of the ravine which they were now climbing. They were very hot, and they had certainly been walking for more than half an hour, but neither of them was eager to turn back. It was an adventure, and Harriet was as keen as Susan to reach their destination.

A clearing among the trees gave them their first glimpse of the chateau. Perched on its crag, it looked more like a castle than ever, its pepperpot turrets and crenellated parapet tinged a golden colour in the sunlight.

Breathing deeply, they plunged upward through the trailing strands of creeper, and emerged on a narrow ledge which appeared to run right round the outer walls of the chateau. The view from here was magnificent, encompassing as it did the jutting roofs of the village above the wider reaches of the river. In the distance, the turrets of another chateau pointed towards the sky, and all around the thickly planted fruit orchards gave an impression of impregnability. The stream seemed to disappear below the chateau, and Harriet was pondering this phenomenon, when Susan exclaimed in a low voice:

'I say, isn't that Paul Laroche?'

Harriet looked round quickly. Sure enough, André's son was sauntering towards them along the narrow path, and short of beating a hasty retreat, there was no way they could avoid him.

'Hi!' he greeted them nonchalantly, a lazy grin spreading over his handsome features. 'I did not know we were to have visitors.'

'You're not,' declared Harriet crisply. 'We just wanted to look at the chateau.'

'Really?' His eyes narrowed appreciatively as they took in the attractive picture she made. '*Bien*, you must let me show you around. The chateau is not generally open to tourists, you understand, but I think we can make an exception in your case, *n'est-ce pas*?'

'We don't expect any favours,' Harriet said shortly, disappointed that they had made the journey for nothing. 'Susan, we'd better be going back—'

'No, wait!' Paul caught her arm, and then released it again when she gave him a pointed stare. 'I mean—please. I would like to show you around.'

Susan looked appealingly at her aunt. 'Couldn't we?' she pleaded. 'After all, we have come a long way. . .'

Harriet sighed. 'This estate is obviously private—'

'Please,' Paul interrupted her. 'There is no need to run away.'

'I'm not running away!' Harriet retorted, glaring at him, and then abruptly looking away from his knowing stare. 'All right. How do we get in?'

'I will show you.'

Paul grinned again, and led them back the way he had come. They followed the curving wall of the chateau, and as they turned away from the ravine, the path widened slightly and became shadowed by trees. A few more yards and they had reached the sweep of parkland that fronted the building; acres of turf which should have been satin-smooth and which were now sadly in need of cutting. Beyond the park were the woods where Harriet imagined previous Counts of Rochefort had hunted for deer and wild boar, but which like the rest of the place had become sadly overgrown.

The chateau itself was bigger than she had expected, with tall iron gates giving on to an inner courtyard. Blank windows and an air of neglect pervaded the atmosphere, but nothing could detract from the warm beauty of the stonework.

'The Chateau de Rochefort!' announced Paul mockingly. 'Four hundred years of history, crumbling into dust.'

'Is it really that old?' Susan was impressed, but Paul shook his head.

'Much of the original structure was rebuilt in the nineteenth century,' he explained, 'but during the war it was occupied by the Germans, and unfortunately it was looted. My grandparents died during the occupation.'

'I'm sorry.'

Harriet offered her sympathy while the realisation ran through her head that at least in that instance, André had told her the truth. But Paul merely shrugged his shoulders in his distinctly Gallic way, and walked towards the iron gates.

'Wait!' Harriet hastened after him. 'We won't go inside.'

'Why not?'

Harriet gestured feebly. 'Is it occupied?'

Paul's brows drew together. 'Only the lodge,' he replied. 'I thought you knew.'

'Knew?' Harriet shook her head. 'Knew what?'

'That we live in the lodge,' Paul said astonishingly, and Harriet wished the ground would open up and swallow her. It was all very well amusing herself by picturing André's reactions to her intrusion into his home, and quite another to anticipate the reality.

'You live in the lodge?' Happily Susan had none of her aunt's inhibitions. 'How exciting!'

Paul bestowed her with a rather patronising look, and then turned to Harriet again. 'What is wrong? Do you not want to see the chateau? I promise you it is not half as—what would you say?—run-down—as it looks.'

Harriet pushed her hair back with a nervous hand. 'It's not that. . .' she was beginning, when

a man came out of the side door of the lodge
and stood looking at them. It was André. She
scarcely needed to look at him to feel the automatic tightening of her stomach muscles, the
almost telepathic awareness of his nearness that
brought the bitterness of aloes to her throat. He
recognised them at once, in spite of the fact that
the sun was in his eyes, and strode purposefully
towards them.

Paul, intercepting her discomfort, glanced
round and pulled a face. '*Bon sang*, Papa!' he
drawled, catching her attention for a moment. 'I
wonder if he knows you are afraid of him!'

'I'm not afraid of him!' Harriet hissed indignantly, and then André was upon them, his dark
eyes narrowing as he overheard the whisper, if
not the actual words, of that heated denunciation.

'This is an unexpected pleasure,' he observed,
looking at Susan, not her aunt. 'Is there something amiss? You have some complaint,
perhaps?'

Harriet was embarrassingly aware of the brev-
ity of her shorts, and of the vaguely sardonic
expression André was wearing. In brown corded
pants and a cream silk shirt, he looked less
approachable somehow, and she resented his
inference. Good lord, did he imagine they had
come looking for *him*? If she had known who
she was going to encounter she would have kept
her distance from Rochefort. Still it occurred to
her that perhaps he was the caretaker of the
chateau, and that would explain how Paul came

to know so much about it. Yet, if he was caretaker, her thoughts ran on, had he really owned
her house, or like some retainers who referred
to property as their own, did he actually mean
it was owned by the estate?

'We wanted to see the chateau,' she heard
Susan saying now. 'It's beautiful, isn't it? I like
that funny little dome over there. Is it a
chimney?'

André cast a fleeting look at the building. 'It's
a bell tower, actually,' he told her with a smile.
'Years ago, at the time of the Revolution, there
was much poverty in the village. My ancestors
kept what you would call a soup-kitchen here,
and anyone who came was given a bowl of soup
and a crust of bread.' His smile grew ironic.
'That unhappily did not prevent them from ulti-
mately losing their heads, but fortunately for me,
their son escaped to England.'

Harriet scarcely registered anything after *My
ancestors. . . His* ancestors! She blinked rapidly.
Did that mean he was the present Comte de
Rochefort?

'Have you got something in your eye, Miss
Ingram?'

Paul's face mirrored his amusement, and she
pressed her lips together angrily. 'No,' she
retorted coldly. 'The sun is very bright,
that's all.'

Patently he didn't believe her, and her words
attracted André's attention, too. 'Perhaps you
would care to take a glass of wine with us, and

then, if you wish, Paul will show you what is left of the chateau,' he suggested, but although Susan looked eager, Harriet shook her head.

'I'm afraid we must be getting back,' she replied curtly, firmly disregarding Susan's disappointment. 'It was further than we anticipated, and I've left the car in a rather awkward spot.'

'You came by car?'

André frowned, and she guessed he really had believed they had come this way deliberately. She hated him for his supreme arrogance, and said the first thing that came into her head.

'We were on our way to Cahors, actually,' she declared, hoping that Susan would not contradict her, and at least she had the satisfaction of knowing she had puzzled him. But it didn't last.

'Are you not going in the wrong direction for Cahors?' he queried politely, and her cheeks flamed when she had to acknowledge that she wasn't sure. 'I think you will find you take the road to Bel-sur-Baux, not Rochelac,' he added, and Harriet hid her resentment.

'I'm very grateful for the information, *monsieur*,' she thanked him tautly, and with a brief nod at Paul would have left them, but André stepped forward.

'You must come and take a drink with us some other time,' he insisted, the expression in his eyes hidden by the narrowing of his lids, and she wondered if he was aware of how much she despised him.

'I shouldn't dream of intruding,' she retorted curtly.

'There would be no intrusion,' he assured her. 'We have few visitors these days.'

Harriet wondered how much of this double-edged conversation Paul understood. She was glad Susan was too young to appreciate the nuances of it, but Paul was regarding them both curiously, and not without some degree of interest.

'You haven't thanked Monsieur Laroche for the furniture!' Susan put in suddenly, and Paul gave a hoot of derision.

'*Monsieur Laroche*!' he mimicked mockingly, and Susan stared at him in hurt surprise.

'What's the matter—'

'Monsieur Laroche!' said Paul again, and pulled a face at Harriet.

That was the last straw. 'If your father has not seen fit to tell us that he is not *Monsieur* Laroche, I see no reason why we should be ridiculed for addressing him as such!' she spat out angrily. 'And if you're an example of the sons of the aristocracy, then I wish them well of you!'

And grasping Susan's arm, she turned the startled girl round and propelled her swiftly back the way they had come.

'Just a minute. . .'

André's hand closing round the yielding flesh of her upper arm brought her to an unwilling standstill. Harriet released Susan abruptly, and she turned, too, staring at André with wide,

frightened eyes. Harriet didn't know which to
tackle first. She wanted to tear André's hard
fingers from her arm and comfort Susan all at
the same time, and she gave André an angry
stare before saying:

'Don't look like that, Sue! No one's going to
hurt you.'

She turned to look at André again, and after
a silent battle of wills, his hand fell to his side.
But his mouth was a thin line and she wondered
if she was being over-optimistic. Of Paul there
was no sign, and for that she was relieved.

André dragged his eyes away from Harriet's
face, and looked at the younger girl. 'I apologise
for my son, Susan,' he said quietly. 'I regret he
has been allowed to run wild these last few years.
He is not used to gentle English girls.'

Susan licked her lips. 'That's all right.' She
looked awkwardly at her aunt. 'Are—are you
coming?'

Harriet was about to agree, when André
spoke again.

'In a moment, Susan. You go on ahead. I wish
to have a private word with your aunt.'

Harriet's head jerked round. 'I don't think we
have anything to say to one another—*Comte*!'
she declared coldly, but this time her eyes fell
before the grim penetration of his. With an irritable little shrug, she nodded and said: 'Go on,
then, Susan. I won't be a minute.'

Susan hesitated a moment longer, and then,
rather uncertainly, she scrambled down the steep

path to the foot of the ravine, and Harriet was left standing with André in the shade of a huge old yew tree.

'Well?' she demanded, as soon as Susan was out of earshot, watching her toe scuffing the parched earth. 'What do you want to say?'

There was silence for so long that it became an almost tangible presence between them, and then at last he spoke.

'I realise this is a difficult situation, Harriet, but it does not help to treat me like a leper!'

'Why not?' She lifted her head defiantly. 'That's what you are, aren't you?'

There was another silence, and then: 'You really hate me, don't you, Harriet?'

He sounded surprised, and her anger erupted once more. 'What did you expect? That I would be thrilled to see you? That I might have forgotten what a selfish swine you really are!'

The muscles of his face tightened at her accusations. She could see a pulse beating erratically at the base of his throat where the opened neck of his shirt revealed the taut bones and sinews of his chest. His skin was brown and oiled with sweat, and betrayingly she remembered the feel of his skin against hers, the hard demanding urgency of his body pressing hers down into the yielding softness of the bed. . .

'If I had been selfish,' he enunciated softly, 'I would have kept you as my mistress! It would have been months—years, *peut-être*, before you found out the truth!'

Harriet trembled uncontrollably. 'Am I supposed to be grateful for that?'

His lips twisted. 'No. Gratitude is obviously not what you feel.'

'Is that all you wanted to say?'

'No!' His fists clenched. 'If possible—I wanted to try and explain—'

'*Explain*!' She took a step back from him. 'What can you explain to me? Leave it! Just leave it—and *me*—alone!'

Her angry eyes lifted to his, but what she saw there brought flaming colour to her throat and spread revealingly up her neck to her face. Dark irises, flecked with amber, displayed a wry disbelief he made no attempt to hide; then his gaze dropped deliberately down the length of her body, lingering with careless insolence on the revealing swell of her breasts clearly outlined against the thin cotton of her top.

Harriet was shocked and embarrassed by the ruthlessness of that appraisal, and taking a deep breath, she exclaimed: 'Don't look at me like that!'

'Like what?' There was no warmth in his voice now, and she had to summon all her courage to go on.

'Like—as if you were—undressing me!' she got out chokingly, and his dark brows lifted mockingly.

'It would not be the first time, would it, *chérie*?' he drawled cruelly.

'You're a—a—'

'Selfish swine is, I think, the going description,' he supplied, 'Very well, Harriet, I get the message. Is that not also the current phrase?'

Harriet sighed, all aggression suddenly going out of her. She bent her head feeling an awful sense of futility, and wondered at the treachery of flesh over spirit. Was she never going to be free of this man?

The sound of his footsteps retreating along the path brought her head up, and a sick lump invaded her throat as she watched him. He was unbuttoning his shirt for coolness, and she saw him flex his shoulder muscles almost wearily.

The urge to run after him was practically irresistible. A terrible weakness spread over her, and she closed her eyes in aching misery. Oh, God, she prayed silently, don't do this to me!

CHAPTER FIVE

THEN a tentative hand touched her arm, and her eyes flicked open to see Susan standing looking anxiously at her.

'Harriet?' she adjured worriedly. 'Is something wrong?'

Harriet looked all about her, and after assuring herself that they were alone, she pushed her hair back from her face. Then she shook her head vigorously, forcing a smile.

'The heat. . .' she murmured vaguely.

Susan looked sceptical now. 'What did Monsieur Laroche say to you? You look awfully pale.'

'I've told you, it's the heat!' Harriet was in no mood to parry words. 'Let's get back to the car. I could do with a drink.'

'Then why didn't you accept Monsieur Laroche's invitation?' exclaimed Susan sulkily, and Harriet knew she would have to give some sort of explanation.

'Look,' she said, in a controlled voice, 'we can't talk here. And in any case, he's not Monsieur Laroche; he's the owner of the chateau—the Comte de Rochefort!'

'Is he?' Susan stared past her, at the walls of the chateau. 'Gosh!' Then she frowned. 'But what would a count be doing cleaning out our firegrate?'

'You might well ask,' retorted Harriet dryly. 'Go on, Susan, get moving! We can't stand here all day.'

Crossing the stream, Harriet permitted herself a moment's reflection. She wondered what explanation André would give his wife if his son chose to tell his mother about their strange visitors. After all, her reaction to the boy's ridicule had been out of all proportion to the offence, and Paul was no fool. But that was his father's problem, she told herself fiercely, refusing to admit the guilt that was threatening to overwhelm her.

Gritting her teeth, she hurried on after Susan. She was the fool, she thought bitterly, allowing André to get under her skin like this. Hadn't she had enough misery because of him? What was she, some kind of masochist who enjoyed flaying herself?

The car was stiflingly hot, and Susan was occupied for a few minutes opening all the windows and fanning herself dramatically. Harriet climbed behind the wheel and reversed out on to the road, turning back towards the house.

'Are we really going to Cahors?' Susan exclaimed, but her aunt shook her head.

'We're going home,' Harriet announced levelly, and thereafter concentrated on her driving to the exclusion of everything else.

But back at the house, it was impossible to avoid a confrontation, and with a feeling of inevitability Harriet went about the task of preparing a salad for lunch, aware of her niece's hovering disfavour.

Susan took up a position in the open doorway, one leg raised to rest her foot against the jamb, and then said irritably: 'Well? Aren't you going to tell me what all that was about?'

Harriet played for time. 'All what?'

Susan sighed. 'Don't give me that. You know what I mean. Exactly how well do you know Monsieur—I mean—the *Count*?'

'Not well at all.' Harriet looked up. 'Susan! I saw some cress when I was down at the stream this morning. Do you think you could get me some?'

Susan's expression became even more mutinous. 'I don't know what's cress and what isn't,' she declared.

Harriet shrugged, drying her hands. 'Never mind, I'll get it myself.' She crossed to the open doorway which let into the little hall which in turn gave access to the back garden. 'We really must get around to cutting this grass. If it rains, we'll get soaked walking through it.'

Susan sniffed. 'So you're not going to tell me.'

'Oh, Susan!' Harriet looked around at her frustratedly. 'You're too young to understand.'

'But you did know him better than you pretended, didn't you?'

'I—went out with him a few times—yes.'

'When was that?'

Harriet coloured. 'Eight years ago.' Susan gave her a speculative little look and her aunt's lips tightened. 'I know,' she said. 'He was a married man. . .'

'. . .with a family,' Susan added, frowning. 'Did you know?'

Harriet wrenched open the door. 'No.'

'But he did,' murmured Susan astutely, and Harriet's head jerked round. 'I'm beginning to understand.'

'Are you?' Harriet doubted it. 'I'll get the cress.'

The following day they went to Cahors. Harriet refused to admit why she had chosen that particular place to visit first except that she was determined not to let André imagine they had gone to the chateau for any other reason than she had stated.

The road to Cahors ran through the hilly country that abounded the valley of the river Lot, and they came upon the town unexpectedly, its towers and fortifications rising above the river in mediaeval splendour. With the Lot flowing on three sides, Harriet guessed it must have formed a natural fortification, and on the fourth the old ramparts ran from east to west, enclosing the town.

There were several bridges across the river, the most spectacular of them being the four-teenth-century Valentre bridge, which was

referred to in some guide books as the most
beautiful bridge in the world. With its huge
Gothic arches and slender towers, it was an
impressive sight, but Harriet had visited Venice,
and for her nothing could equal the beauty of
the Rialto's white arches and the pretty little
pavilion that sat on top. But Susan had never
been to Italy, and consequently was less critical.
She took several photographs before they moved
on to the cathedral, and Harriet half envied her
lack of sophistication.

Afterwards they had their lunch at a pavement
bistro in a side street near the river. Plane trees
shaded the tables, and although Harriet was tired
she felt more relaxed than she had done for days.
They ate crusty bread and pâté washed down
by a local wine, with the melodic sound of an
accordion mingling with the harsher sounds of
energetic conversation. No one was in any hurry
to clear the tables, and the lunchtime hours
drifted lazily into afternoon.

Later, they shopped for souvenirs in the
Boulevard Gambetta, and then made their way
back to the car for the drive home. Susan exam-
ined her thin limbs critically as she clambered
into the seat beside Harriet, and smiling
exclaimed:

'Do you remember when you went into that
shop to buy some bread? Well, while I was
standing outside a boy actually winked at me!
What do you think of that?'

Harriet laughed. 'I told you it was only a matter of time.' She pulled a serious face. 'I trust you didn't acknowledge it.'

'I blushed,' admitted Susan honestly, and Harriet chuckled as she started the car.

It was good to get back in spite of everything. Harriet climbed out of the car and stretched luxuriously, pleasantly weary after the long drive. Susan got out too, and while Harriet was collecting their sweaters from the back of the car, she took the keys and went to open the door.

'Hey, you've got some mail!' she exclaimed, bending to pick up an envelope that was lying just inside the door, and Harriet strolled up the path to meet her, raising her eyebrows.

'It's got no stamp!' declared Susan, frowning. 'And there's something heavy inside.'

Feeling the threads of tension closing about her once more, Harriet reached for the envelope and abruptly slit it open. There was a piece of paper inside, but it had no writing on it. It was simply the wrapping for the key which fell noisily on to the stones at their feet as Harriet unfolded it.

Susan bent and picked it up, looking at it in surprise. Then she looked at her aunt. 'It's the spare key, isn't it?' she ventured awkwardly. 'The one—the one the Count said he had.'

Harriet nodded, brushing past her to go into the kitchen. 'It looks like it,' she agreed tautly, and Susan followed her inside without making any further comment.

*   *   *

Two days later, Harriet was upstairs making beds when the sound of voices brought her curiously to the window. They had had no visitors, if you could discount André and his son, and she wondered who Susan could be talking to.

She was not left long in doubt. The lazily confident tones were those of Paul Laroche, and hearing Susan's nervous laugh, Harriet guessed he was using all his charm on her impressionable niece. No doubt Susan herself was enjoying the opportunity to exercise her newly-discovered felinity, and certainly Paul was an attractive animal on whom to try her claws. He was a younger, less sophisticated edition of his father, and remembering what his father had done sent Harriet hurrying down the stairwell.

Susan looked rather disappointed at her aunt's appearance. She was lounging on the edge of the kitchen table in a fair imitation of a model displaying the latest in sun-tan lotion on legs that were bare below the scanty cover of cuffed shorts. With her profile turned towards him, she was making the most of her other attributes, but judging from Paul's expression, Harriet guessed he had seen it all before. Unlike her niece, he seemed relieved at her interruption, and only as admiration deepened the intensity of his regard did Harriet realise she was still only wearing the navy blue bikini she had worn to bathe earlier. Since the day André had appeared while she was bathing, she had been chary of taking off all her clothes in the stream, and she always kept her bikini on hand for emergencies.

'Good morning,' Paul greeted her politely, his manner belied by his expression. 'How nice to see you again.'

Susan straightened, a look of defiance replacing her previous good humour. 'Paul's asked me to go and play tennis with him,' she said before Harriet could say anything. 'You don't mind, do you, Aunt Harriet?'

In spite of her annoyance that the Laroches appeared to think they could come and go as they pleased, Harriet couldn't help a moment's amusement at Susan's unsubtle attempt to define their relationship. Even so, she could not approve the request, and she crossed the room to fill the kettle for no other reason than to avoid the girl's half guilty stare.

'Where do you plan to play?' she asked, above the sound of water running into the kettle, but before Susan could reply, Paul interposed himself between them so that although Harriet could see his face, Susan couldn't.

'There are grass courts at the chateau,' he told her, his gaze frankly appraising. 'Why do you not come, too?'

Harriet felt an unwilling response to his undoubtedly sensual attraction. He was so like André, and she looked down abstractedly when the kettle overflowed, spilling water on to the stone floor.

'Damn!' she swore impatiently, reaching for a cloth, but Paul was there before her, taking the cloth and mopping the flags about her feet with easy competence. Once the cloth brushed her toes and she looked down quickly as he looked up. Their eyes met, and she knew without a shadow of doubt that he had touched her deliberately.

His behaviour irritated her, not least because he was a boy of sixteen, while she was ten years his senior and should surely have been beyond his influence.

Whether Susan was aware of the exchange of glances, Harriet did not know, but the kettle clanged noisily as she set it on the gas ring, and attracted the girl's attention.

'Well?' she asked. 'Can I go?'

Harriet caught her lower lip between her teeth, avoiding looking at Paul. Then she made an indifferent gesture: 'I can't stop you, if that's what you want to do.'

Susan drew a sharp breath. 'Oh, good! I could do with the exercise.' She turned to Paul, who was now lounging against the table himself. 'Just give me a minute, and I'll get my racquet.'

Her cork soles clattered away up the stairs, and left alone with the boy Harriet felt ridiculously embarrassed. To banish the feeling she deliberately walked outside, raising her face to the glory of the morning, and then sighed frustratedly when she realised he had followed her and was standing right behind her.

'*Tu es belle!*' he said, in a low voice, not looking at her, but bending to pull a blade of

grass, so that she thought for a moment she had
imagined his words. Then, as he straightened
and looked at her, she knew she had not.

'You shouldn't say things like that to me!'
she declared crossly, passing the palms of her
hands over her hot cheeks. 'I—don't like it.'

'*Pas possible!*'

'I do.'

'*Pourquoi? C'est vrai!*'

'*Paul!*'

She said his name a trifle desperately, but
when his fingers reached out to stroke the
smooth length of her arm, she hastily put some
distance between them. He moved his shoulders
inconsequently, his arms tanned and muscular
beyond the short sleeves of his sweat shirt. He
was easily as tall as Harriet herself, and she
thought how much older he seemed than boys
of his age in England.

'I like the way you say my name, Harriet,' he
murmured, chewing the blade of grass as he
covered the space she had opened. Then: 'Why
do you not come with us? You know that is why
I came.'

Harriet decided this had gone far enough. It
was one thing to feel a certain amount of flattery
at the boy's evident admiration, and quite
another to permit him familiarities denied to men
twice his age.

'I think you're getting out of your depth,
darling,' she told him, deliberately using a patronising tone, and was relieved to see from his

change of expression that her barb appeared to
have struck home. But what he might have said
or done next was denied to her by Susan's
appearance in the doorway, and Paul was forced
to turn away.

'I'm ready!'

Susan's voice was young and innocent, and
suddenly Harriet realised exactly what she might
be letting her in for. How could a girl of Susan's
age cope with a boy like Paul, for in spite of
his youth he was obviously not without some
experience. Exactly how much, Harriet would
rather not know.

'It's after eleven, you know,' she said now,
and Paul cast her a speculative glance. 'Isn't it
a little too near lunchtime? Won't it be too hot
to play tennis?'

Susan's mouth grew sulky. 'You said you
didn't mind!' she protested.

'Correction: I said I couldn't stop you,'
declared her aunt dryly. She walked back across
the grass to the door, then turned provocative
eyes in Paul's direction. 'You once said that
perhaps you might be of some assistance to us?'
He acknowledged this silently, and she went on:
'Maybe this is your opportunity. The grass needs
cutting.'

'Harriet!'

Susan's mutinous cry went unnoticed by Paul,
as with a lazy smile, he said: 'If you need my
assistance, how can I refuse?'

Harriet wished he could have chosen more

tactful words to accept her offer, and Susan uttered another hurt ejaculation before turning and marching back into the house. Harriet looked after her anxiously, wondering whether she had done more harm than good by stopping the child from going with him, but then she looked at Paul again and decided she had done the most sensible thing. But how long could she keep them apart if Paul chose to use Susan as a weapon against her?

'What do I use to cut the grass?' he asked now, and Harriet looked at him irritably.

'You really don't give a damn about anybody, do you?' she demanded hotly.

'No?' He sounded indignant. 'I am going to cut your grass, am I not?'

'Because it suits you!'

'No.' He shook his head. 'Because it suits you.' He grinned. 'Now, what do I use? Your tongue?'

Harriet suppressed a wilful smile. 'There's a scythe in the shed at the back of the house,' she told him shortly, and not giving him chance to say anything more, she followed Susan into the house.

She found the girl in the bedroom, stretched out on her bed, sobbing as if her heart would break. Harriet stood hesitantly at the head of the stairs, looking over her shoulder doubtfully, and then, with a sigh, she moved to the bed.

'Susan. . .' There was no reply, and she sank down on to the edge of the mattress. 'Susan.'

But Susan just scrambled away from her, getting off the bed at the other side and going to stand tremulously before the dressing table.

'Oh, Susan,' exclaimed Harriet frustratedly, 'stop looking at me like that! I'm not some kind of monster, you know. I—I just did what I thought was best.'

'For you!' declared Susan bitterly. 'I thought you said he was too young!'

'What?' Harriet uttered a sound of disbelief. 'He is Susan, for God's sake don't imagine I was jealous!'

'You were! You were! You thought he should have asked you!'

'That's nonsense!' exclaimed Harriet in exasperation. 'I've got no desire to play tennis in the heat of the day! Go swimming, perhaps. But not play tennis!'

'That's what you say!'

'I mean it.' Harriet rose to her feet. 'Susan, listen to me!' She lowered her voice in case Paul could hear them through the open window. 'Paul Laroche may be too young for me, but he's too old for you!'

'He's not. He's only sixteen—he told me. I'll be fifteen in December!'

Harriet cast her eyes heavenward for a moment. 'Age isn't only a matter of years, Susan. You must know experience is what counts!'

Susan rubbed her nose with the back of her

hand. 'And you're an expert on these things, I suppose.'

'Oh, Susan!'

Harriet stared at her helplessly, but Susan was not prepared to give in. 'It's all right for you,' she muttered, 'you like lounging about all the time. But I don't. I'm young. I wanted to do something different. And just because you weren't invited, you're pretending—'

'I *was* invited!' stated Harriet unwillingly.

Susan looked up. 'You weren't!'

'I was.' Harriet heaved a sigh. 'Paul invited me. After you'd gone to get ready.'

Susan stared at her suspiciously. 'I don't believe you.'

Harriet shrugged wearily. 'Ask him.'

Susan absorbed this in silence for a few moments, then her lips pursed. 'Even so—'

'Even so, nothing, Susan. Look, I don't want to stop you from making friends. If some girl or boy of your own age came along, I'd be the first to encourage you.'

'Paul *is* my age!'

Harriet shook her head. 'Oh, well, if you won't listen to me. . .' She turned back towards the stairs, and then remembering her state of undress, went instead to the *armoire* and pulled out a denim skirt and matching tie-waisted blouse. Susan watched her put them on without speaking, but when Harriet made a final attempt to appeal to her, turned away to lean her elbows on the window frame, looking down provocatively into the garden. Feeling defeated, Harriet went slowly downstairs.

Paul was swinging the scythe in the back garden. He had taken off his shirt and the bronzed skin showed he often went without it. He had already cleared a patch about six feet square, and sweat was rolling off him.

Reluctantly, Harriet acknowledged he was working hard, and going to stand at the door, she asked: 'Would you like a drink?'

Paul straightened, flexing his spine, and grinned at her. 'Would I not!'

Harriet inclined her head, and turning, went back into the kitchen. They had no refrigerator, and for coolness, she kept cans of Coke and bitter lemon on a section of the stone floor where the sun never reached. She picked up a glass, weighed it in her hand, and then put it down again. She had the feeling Paul would prefer it from the can.

He came towards her when she reappeared, and she held the Coke out at arm's length. 'I have bitter lemon, if you prefer it,' she said crisply, but he shook his head, taking the can and raising it to his lips. He swallowed half the contents at a gulp, and then wiped his mouth on the back of his hand.

'*Bien!*' he said, reverting to French as he always did when they were alone. Then: 'Why have you covered yourself up? You should be glad you can wear a bikini. Lots of girls cannot.'

'You mean—of my age?' suggested Harriet

dryly, and his sweat-streaked face flushed with colour.

'Why do you say things like that?' he demanded, and for once she could see he was serious.

Turning adroitly aside, she waved a careless arm and said: 'You're doing well. I'm very grateful.'

He shrugged, finishing the Coke, and then tossed the empty can in his hand. 'You think I am playing a game, no?' he murmured.

Harriet sighed. 'I think you're being very silly,' she declared shortly. 'Does your father know you're here?'

'Does it matter?'

'I think so.'

'Why?' He put down the can and moved back to his task. 'Because you think he would not approve?' He paused. 'Or because you do not wish to make him jealous?'

Harriet's breath caught in her throat. 'I don't know what you're talking about.'

'No?' He straightened once more, and looked across at her. 'But you do know my father, do you not?'

'I'm too busy to stand here fencing words with you!' she told him shortly, and turning, went back into the house.

She was shelling peas when Susan appeared. She came moodily into the kitchen, scuffing her toes, and refused to meet her aunt's eyes.

'Is it all right if I go and *talk* to Paul?' she

asked insolently, and Harriet shrugged her shoulders.

'Please yourself,' she retorted, in no mood to humour the girl, and Susan flounced outside without another word.

It was nearly a quarter to one when Paul appeared at the kitchen door, his long hair hanging in damp strands about his shoulders. 'The lawn at the back is finished,' he announced, wiping a greasy hand across his forehead. 'It needs trimming with a mower, but you do not have one, do you?' Harriet shook her head, and he nodded. 'I can come back tomorrow if you like and do the grass at the front.'

'Oh, Paul!' Harriet left what she was doing to look sympathetically at him. 'You must be exhausted!' She glanced behind her. 'Do you—well, would you like to stay and have lunch with us?'

His eyes disturbed her, but she maintained her composure, and he said at last: 'I think I had better go back. Louise will be wondering where I am.' *That name again!* 'Do you want me to come tomorrow?'

'I—we might not be here tomorrow,' she murmured evasively. 'We—were thinking of going to Beynac.'

'Beynac.' He nodded thoughtfully. 'Well, if you are not here, it does not matter.'

Harriet shifted uncomfortably. 'I—I feel as though I should pay you. . .' she protested, and his eyes narrowed.

'Susan said you liked swimming. Come swimming with me the day after.'

'Paul—'

'And Susan, of course,' he added irrepressibly, and she stared at him in aggravation.

'Where could we go swimming?' she demanded.

'In the river. I know a place where the water is deep and the trees are shady.'

'You've been there many times before, I suppose,' remarked Harriet wryly, and he grinned appealingly.

'Say you will come.'

'I'll think about it.'

Paul reached for his sweat shirt and pulled it on over his head. 'I will be here about eleven. The day after tomorrow.' He paused. 'And tomorrow—whether you are here or not.'

As it happened, it rained next day. Not a drizzle like they might have expected in England, but a steady downpour that fell like a grey curtain around the house, soaking the grass and trees alike, and putting the idea of sightseeing out of the question.

Harriet was disappointed, not least because her relationship with Susan still bordered on a state of armed truce, and she had hoped a trip out together might relieve the situation. But it was not to be, and Susan spent most of the day lounging about the *salon* reading while Harriet experimented with the cooker, producing a batch of cakes that tasted as good as they looked. But her heart was not in it, and she thought wryly that she was behaving more like Susan's mother than her aunt.

Happily, it was fine the next day, and Harriet was still in her dressing gown when there was a knock at the door. She peered through the window before opening the door, and gave an exclamation of impatience when she saw Paul standing outside.

'You're early!' she exclaimed, after she had unlocked the door, and he acknowledged the truth of this.

'I wanted to get the grass cut early,' he said simply. 'We have a date at eleven.'

Harriet gave him a resigned look. 'All right,' she agreed. 'But don't imagine we're going to make a habit of this. I'll come with you this time, but. . .' She shook her head. 'You know where the scythe is.'

Paul sniffed appreciatively. 'Are you not going to offer me some coffee?' he protested, but she just shook her head, and closed the door in his face.

Susan came down the stairs blinking. She must have heard their voices because she had taken the trouble to put on jeans and a tee-shirt, and she looked round in surprise when she found her aunt was alone.

'Paul's here,' remarked Harriet reluctantly. 'He's going to cut the grass at the front of the house.'

Susan went to the window and looked out. 'Where is he?'

'I imagine he's getting the scythe,' replied Harriet, pouring herself some coffee. She hesitated, and then added: 'Do you fancy going swimming later?'

Susan turned. 'Swimming? Where?'

Harriet cradled her cup between her fingers, looking down into it to avoid looking at the girl. 'Paul says he knows a place. He's invited us—both.'

Susan's chin jutted. 'Has he?'

Harriet was forced to look up. 'Yes.'

Susan challenged her gaze. 'What if I don't want to go swimming?'

Harriet's fingers tightened round the cup. 'Don't you?'

Susan pursed her lips. 'No. No, I don't.'

Harriet's heart sank. 'Oh, Susan!'

'What are you going to do now? Go without me?'

'Susan, stop this! I won't have it.'

'What're you going to do about it? You can't force me to go swimming. Besides. . .'

'Besides what?'

'I can't swim.'

Harriet gasped incredulously, 'You—can't—swim?'

'No.' Susan was sullen. 'I was never any good at it.'

'But didn't they teach you at school?'

'They tried to, but I never made it. I guess

I'm just one of those people who can't.'

'Oh, nonsense! Everyone can swim if they try.' Harriet put down her coffee and walked restlessly across the floor. Then she turned. 'Susan, you know I don't want to go with him on my own.'

Susan shrugged annoyingly. 'That's not my problem.'

Harriet could have slapped her, but she had to admire her, too. She had certainly turned the tables very successfully. Was she aware of *how* successfully?

Deciding there was no point in appealing to her better nature, Harriet washed her face and hands at the sink, cleaned her teeth, and then ran upstairs to get dressed. Somehow she had to think of a way out of this, but right now she felt completely at a loss to know what to do.

CHAPTER SIX

WHEN she came downstairs again the door was open and Susan had disappeared. Guessing she had gone to talk to Paul, Harriet gulped down her now cold coffee, and carried her dirty cup to the sink. She glanced at her watch. Nine o'clock! She had two hours to find an excuse not to accompany him.

It was too nice a morning to stay indoors, and she stepped outside, breathing deeply, loving the scent of the mimosa that grew in such profusion beneath the windows. Paul was some distance away, swinging the scythe rhythmically, as he cleared the tangle of weeds and grasses that grew under the hedge. But of Susan there was no sign.

As usual when he saw her, Paul straightened and called: 'Another hour should be enough.'

Harriet nodded, looking about her half anxiously. 'Have you seen Susan?'

'Yes. She told me to tell you she has gone for a walk,' Paul explained, and Harriet felt a quivering impatience. So she had left to it, had she? Well, two could play at that game!

Paul was still looking at her, and on impulse she exclaimed: 'Do you want a drink now?'

He aimed the scythe at the turf, and it landed with a thud, projecting from the soil like some giant question mark. Then he wiped his hands down the seat of his jeans and crossed the grass towards her.

Harriet retreated into the house, half regretting her impulsive offer, but it was too late now. He was coming in through the door, pushing his damp hair back from his forehead.

She lifted a can from the corner, saw it was bitter lemon, and went to change it. She dropped the tin of Coke she took up instead, and swore softly to herself as she rescued it again. Paul watched this small tableau with interest, and came to stand beside her as she pulled unavailingly at the ring opener.

'Let me do it,' he offered, but she shook her head, tugging viciously at the loop of metal until it gave without warning, splashing cold Coke over Paul's chest.

He gasped, clutching at himself dramatically, and the tension was relieved as she burst out laughing. She laughed until there were tears in her eyes, and Paul snatched up the can and advanced menacingly upon her, threatening to pour the remains of the Coke over her head.

She was backing off him, still laughing, when she suddenly realised something was obstructing the light from the doorway. She looked past Paul and then felt the familiar constriction of her senses that always occurred when she saw André. Her altered expression conveyed her feelings to Paul. He took a moment to glance round, and then with an exclamation of resignation he gave up the game and setting the can down on the table, faced his father.

André straightened from his lounging position against the jamb, and Harriet had a moment to wonder exactly how long he had been standing there. Then he stepped into the room and she saw to her astonishment that Susan was just behind him.

'What are you doing here, Paul?' he enquired, speaking in English for Susan's benefit. 'I understood Louise to say that you were undertaking part-time employment.'

'I am.'

Paul thrust his hands into the low belt of his jeans, and aware of his belligerence, Harriet hastened to agree with him.

'Your son has been very kind,' she averred coolly. 'He has cut the grass for us—back and front.'

André frowned. 'Is that so?'

'Yes, it is.' Paul took up an aggressive attitude, his gaze flickering scornfully over the girl who was standing behind his father. 'Has someone been telling you differently?'

Susan's mouth twitched, but she said nothing, and Harriet realised with dismay that Paul had hit on the truth.

'Oh, Susan!' she exclaimed. 'You didn't!' But she could tell from her niece's flushed face that she had.

André's nostrils flared. 'Your niece came to tell me that my son was here,' he said quietly, and Harriet wondered how much he was omitting. 'Paul! Your great-grandmother is waiting for you to take her for a walk. Perhaps Miss Ingram will permit you to finish her lawn another day.'

Harriet looked embarrassed now. 'I didn't know that. Paul, you should have told me!'

'You do not believe that, do you?' Paul demanded angrily, but his father's hand descended on his shoulder and although he shook it off, he muttered: 'All right, all right, I am going!'

He winked at Harriet, cast a killing look at Susan, and then walked out of the kitchen, snatching up his shirt as he went down the path. Susan looked after him, her lips trembling uncontrollably, but Harriet couldn't altogether feel sympathetic towards her. She had actually gone to the chateau and brought André back here with the sole intention of preventing them from going swimming together. There was something rather malicious about the whole business.

'I think you'd better go upstairs, Susan,' she declared, and with a petulant sniff the girl rushed across the room and up the stairs, banging the door behind her.

Left alone with André, Harriet looked at him uncomfortably, not quite knowing why he had stayed and wondering whether he expected her to apologise. Like his son, he was wearing denims, but instead of a shirt he had on a sleeveless waistcoat that exposed the powerful muscles of his arms. He had obviously been working, for there were smudges of dirt on his face, and his hands were far from clean.

When he made no move to go, Harriet took a deep breath and said: 'I'm—sorry if Paul has been neglecting his family—'

'Are you?' She got no further as his anger erupted. 'What are you trying to do to me, Harriet? Coming here—living in my house! Expecting me to disregard your presence here as I would a stranger! What do you think I am made of? *Wood?*'

His attack was so unexpected that Harriet was unprepared for it. 'I didn't invite you here!' she protested, with a semblance of indignation, but André wasn't listening to her. His eyes were devouring her, raking the hot colour in her cheeks, flickering over quivering lips and slender throat to linger on the revealing firmness of her breasts. Harriet could feel the nipples hardening, betraying her perturbation to his ruthless appraisal. When his eyes dropped lower, she turned abruptly away from him, unable to withstand the studied sensuality of his gaze, and said in a low voice: 'I think you'd better go.'

'Why?' he demanded, and when he spoke she realised he had covered the space between them and was standing right behind her. 'If my son is welcome here, why should I not be?'

'No—'

Her instinctive protest spoken over her shoulder died in a gasp as he reached for her. The

wall was behind her, and as she tried to back
away from him, she came up against the newly-
painted plaster. It was cool—cool against her
legs, against the backs of her arms, against the
creamy skin of her midriff that stretched between
the blouse tied under her breasts and the denim
shorts that circled her hips. And her skin was
hot—hot and yet clammy as panic brought a
film of perspiration out all over her. She could
feel its dampness in her palms, along her spine,
between her legs.

Then his mouth was on hers, forcing her head
back against the wall. She felt weak, unable to
fight him as she knew she should, conscious
only of his chest crushing her breasts, making
them ache with a longing to be free of the confin-
ing influence of the blouse, of the swelling
muscles of his thighs straining against hers. His
whole weight was against her, his body fitting
to hers as if it had been made for that purpose,
as it had always been made. . .

'Harriet,' he groaned, loosening the ties of her
blouse, his mouth hungrily seeking the throbbing
curve of her breast.

Harriet's legs trembled. The scent of his body,
the heat and the strength and the hardness of
him was rapidly overwhelming her. He had
always had this effect on her, and the passage
of years had only served to make her woman's
body more responsive to the demands of his. No
other man had ever held her like this, touched
her like this, and the blood in her veins ran

molten, like liquid fire. She wanted him, she realised despairingly, just as she had always done. . .

The floor above creaked as Susan moved restlessly around, and the sound brought Harriet to her senses. In God's name, she thought, horror-stricken, hadn't she suffered enough pain at this man's hands? What was she thinking of, letting him near her like this? Was she completely out of her mind? And apart from anything else, Susan could come down here at any moment.

'No,' she said, in an undertone. Then more clearly: 'No!'

Her hands, which moments before had been spread across the moist flesh of his back, balled into fists and dug into him. She struggled free of him, trembling fingers fastening the blouse in place, agonised eyes avoiding his.

Obviously André wasn't used to having his women pull out on him. He let her go without too much effort, lying back against the wall where she had lain moments before. He stared at her through eyes that were still glazed by the force of his emotions, but there was no mistaking the contempt that pulled down the corners of his mouth.

'Please,' she said, disguising the tremor in her voice, all too potently aware of the power he had exercised over her, 'I want you to go. Now!'

His eyebrows lifted mockingly. 'Why? It is a little late to pretend you did not want that just as much as I did, is it not?'

'Get out!'

He made no move to go, merely straightened away from the wall and ran a hand over the curls of dark hair on his chest that arrowed their way down to his navel. 'A very—interesting, if rather unsatisfying interlude,' he said, but the mockery was cold. 'What did you expect of me, Harriet, I wonder? You should know by now I am no— gentleman, no?'

'Yes, I should,' she cried bitterly. 'Oh, will you just go!'

'So you can console yourself with the thought that you did not succumb this time?' he demanded harshly, stepping towards her so that she backed away again in alarm. 'Oh, relax, Harriet! I have had my lesson for today. Never let it be said that a Laroche does not know when to give in! But do not imagine you can play those sort of games with me. You have got away with it this time, but only because I chose to *let* you!'

Harriet swallowed convulsively. 'I—I don't know how you dare say such a thing!' she declared. 'I—' she licked her dry lips, 'I never want to see you again, do you understand? *Never!*'

His eyes darkened angrily. 'You are a fool, Harriet,' he stated savagely, and without another word, he turned and strode out of the house.

After he had gone, Harriet moved around on legs that seemed too weak to support her. She had never experienced such a scene, and the memory of it refused to be dislodged. Had she invited it? Had she by her behaviour sparked off the latent desire between them? More importantly, had she revealed the emotion he could still arouse in her, the pulsing urgent emotion that once before had traitorously betrayed her? Her body still throbbed from the demanding pressure of his, and she wrapped her arms closely about herself, willing the treacherous memories away.

A sound on the stairs brought her round with a start to see Susan lurking just beyond the half-open door. Anger at the realisation that the girl had been responsible for the scene that had just taken place was quickly replaced by impatience at her own weakness. How could she blame Susan for what had happened? How could she blame anyone but herself?

'Oh, come in, do!' she said now, half impatiently, and Susan stepped down into the kitchen, the reddened state of her eyes witness to her own misery.

'Harriet?' she said huskily, and then clearing her throat, more firmly: 'Harriet, I'm—I'm sorry.'

Harriet wondered what she was pleading sorry for: bringing André here? Or the scene which had erupted after his arrival?

Now Harriet endeavoured to act naturally. Raising both hands to her head, she smoothed the silky hair behind her ears, and then said briskly: 'So you should be. But it's done with now, and at least—' Her voice almost broke, but she saved it just in time: 'At least I don't have to go swimming now.'

Susan hovered near the staircase door. 'Did— did you want to go?'

Harriet sighed. 'I think we've gone into that, Susan. I think we'd better do some gardening, don't you?'

Swinging the scythe was good therapy. Susan gathered up the cut grass and dumped it in a heap in the back garden, while Harriet did the actual cutting. But it was hot work, and they gave up to bathe in the stream, allowing the crystal-cold water to flow over them. It had been a long morning, Harriet thought, but it was going to be an even longer afternoon.

'You've got a bruise,' Susan observed that night as her aunt undressed for bed, and Harriet quickly donned the cotton top of her pyjamas. She had several, she knew, and she had no desire to discuss their origins with Susan.

But once between the sheets, and under the cover of darkness, her own fingers probed the tender areas around her breast and arms. She could almost feel the calloused hardness of André's hands upon her skin, the lean strength of his fingers digging into her flesh. It brought back with almost lucid clarity every detail of what had happened that morning, and to her shame, her body reacted anew to the remembered masculinity of his. . .

It was possible during the following days to find periods of time when she could delude herself into thinking that the worst was over. She and André had had the confrontation, which from the minute she had seen him she had guessed would come, and now it was up to get on with her life and put all thoughts of the Laroches out of her head. But in moments of relaxation, their intrusion could not be suppressed, and sleep became more of an achievement than a necessity.

Susan was more than willing to meet her half way. She obviously regretted what she had done, and although she could have no real knowledge of the hornet's nest she had stirred up, she was perceptive enough to know that the scene she had motivated had had repercussions she could never have dreamed of. Harriet sometimes wondered whether the girl had guessed what was going on downstairs, or did she simply imagine they had been rowing the whole time? If only they had, she thought bitterly. How much easier it would have been to forget.

But they had come to the Dordogne to see something of the area and, determinedly, Harriet set about doing just that. They visited Rocamadour, rising with precipitate grace above the Alzou Canyon; Sarlat, whose yellow walls and white tiles were so distinctive; Perigueux, capital of Perigord, with its domed cathedral and beautiful old buildings; and finally Bergerac, where they toured the vineyard and tasted some of the wine that made the town famous. The most memorable journey, Harriet felt, was to the caves at Peche-Merle. Dipping into the cliffs for more than two miles, the galleries and vast chambers were a speleologist's dream, containing as they did drawings of animals that had walked the earth some forty thousand years before. Mammoths and bison, stalagmites, and mysterious hand prints, cave pearls that changed in colour from shining white calcite to lustrous red-ochre, because of the presence of iron oxide in the limestone. It was even possible to see the petrified footprint of some prehistoric man, preserved forever in deposits of wet carbonate clay. It was all rather overwhelming, and Harriet emerged with an increased awareness of her own mortality. If only one could apply the lessons learned to one's own life, she thought ruefully, realising how unimportant her problems must seem when set against such a time scale.

About a week after her disastrous encounter with André, Harriet was shopping in Rochelac one morning when she almost collided with Paul. She had just emerged from the patisserie; the sun was in her eyes and she was groping for her dark glasses when a tall figure loomed up in front of her, and she had started to apologise when he said:

'Hello, Harriet.'

'Paul!' She pushed her sunglasses on to her nose and stared at him, half aghast. 'Paul.' She was uneasy now. 'This is a surprise.'

'Is it not?' He glanced round questionably. 'You are alone?'

'Oh.' Harriet shifted her basket from one arm to the other. 'Well, yes. Susan's sunbathing. The weather's been so—marvellous.'

'Yes, it has.' He tucked his thumbs into the hip pockets of his jeans, apparently quite content to stand and look at her with half the population of Rochelac milling interestedly about them. Of course, Harriet thought uncomfortably, these people would know who he was.

Forcing a smile, she said: 'Well, it's been nice seeing you again, Paul—'

'Come and have a Coke with me,' he invited. 'Or a coffee, if you would prefer.'

Harriet gave a regretful shake of her head. 'I—don't think so...'

'Why not? You owe me something, remember?'

Did she not? Harriet moved awkwardly. 'Paul, you know this is not a good idea...'

'Because of my father, I know.' He paused. 'He told me.'

'Told you?' Harriet was horrified. 'Told you what?'

'That you knew one another some years ago: that you do not like him.'

Dear God! Harriet felt quite weak. Was that what André had told his son? Was that what he had told his wife?

'Well then. . .' she began, only to have him interrupt her again.

'My father is not here.' He shrugged indifferently. 'He need never know. And if he does. . .' He spread his hands inconsequently.

Harriet still hesitated. 'Paul, I'm sure there's some other girl who's simply dying for you to ask her for a date—'

His expression darkened irritably. 'Like Susan, I suppose.'

Harriet sighed. 'All right, all right. I'll have a coffee with you.'

'*Bien!*' The irritation disappeared, and he fell into step beside her as they walked towards Monsieur Macon's café. 'So—how are you?'

Harriet couldn't prevent a rueful smile. 'I should say no better for seeing you,' she commented dryly, and then relented when he looked hurt. 'No. I'm fine, thank you. How about you?'

There were tables set outside the café taking full advantage of the brilliant sunshine, and Paul chose one of these, ordering their drinks from a young waitress who gave his companion a more than thorough appraisal before going to get their order.

'Someone else you know?' inquired Harriet mischievously, resting her elbows on the table, and Paul had the grace to look embarrassed for a moment.

'Lise?' He pulled a face. 'She does not have a lot up here.' He tapped his head significantly. 'Now you. . .'

'Forget about me,' advised Harriet crisply. 'Tell me,' she added, changing the subject, 'did you take your great-grandmother for her walk?'

'Louise?' Paul said the name affectionately. 'Yes, I took her.'

Harriet couldn't resist the question: 'Louise? That's your great-grandmother's name?'

Paul nodded. 'Louise Marie-Thérèse Laroche. My father's grandmother.'

'I see.'

'Would you like to meet her?'

'Oh, no!' Hastily Harriet shook her head. That was the last thing she wanted. 'I mean—I wouldn't dream of—of—'

'—visiting my father's house?'

Harriet sighed. 'Something like that. Oh, good, here's the coffee. Hmm, it smells delicious.'

The arrival of the waitress at least provided a respite from Paul's too-shrewd assimilations, and she assumed an intense interest in the contents of her cup.

'Papa said you live in London,' Paul remarked suddenly, and she was forced to look up.

'Did he?' She shrugged. 'Yes, I do, as it happens.'

Paul rested his arms on the table. 'I expect you meet a lot of interesting people in the course of your work.'

'Some,' she admitted, feeling herself to be on firmer ground. 'Why? Are you interested in antiques?'

Paul shook his head. 'No!' He was vehement. 'But I would like to live in London.'

Harriet looked down into her coffee cup again. 'You wouldn't like it,' she assured him firmly.

'How can you say that?' He looked indignant now. 'London is the place to go if you want to be famous.'

'There are more people in London who are not.'

Paul sighed. 'Perhaps they do not have ambition.'

'And you do?'

He nodded vigorously. 'Of course.'

Harriet frowned. 'What would you do in London?'

'Get a job—play my guitar.'

'Oh, I see.' She nodded, her frown clearing. 'You play the guitar. Well, let me tell you, Paul, there are hundreds of boys just like you in London—'

'That is what my father says,' exclaimed Paul impatiently. 'But he does not understand. I am good! I know I am. If I could go to London—get a job with a band—'

'Why not Paris?'

Paul hunched his shoulders. 'I want to go to London.'

Harriet finished her coffee. 'I really must be going now,' she said, taking her purse out of her basket, but seeing her, Paul intervened.

'I will pay,' he told her flatly, and she made no further protest.

The small square was busier than ever, and Harriet explained that she had parked her car on the outskirts of the village. 'Thank you for the coffee,' she said, in what she realised were faintly patronising tones, but Paul was not so easily dismissed.

'I will walk with you,' he insisted, and she had little choice but to agree. The sun was very hot, and her clothes were soon sticking to her, but she maintained the pace in an effort to show the boy she had no desire to linger. She wondered what Charles' reaction would be if he could see her now—walking through Rochelac with *André's* son.

The car was soon reached, and she unlocked it quickly, thrusting her basket on to the back seat. Paul pushed his hands into his pockets, and stood waiting. Harriet summoned another smile, and opened the offside door.

'Well. . .' she said encouragingly, 'I'll say goodbye.'

Paul turned his face up to the sun. 'It's so hot!' he declared.

Harriet cleared her throat. 'Yes.'

'My father is working. Why do you not come to the lodge and meet Louise?'

Harriet's heart sank. 'I—can't.'

'You will not see my father, I promise. They are harvesting the fruit and he is away all day.'

Harriet sought for an excuse. 'Why aren't you helping him?'

Paul grimaced. 'This is my—how do you

say—rest day? Besides, working in the fields is not good for my hands.'

Harriet determinedly got into the car. 'I'm sorry, Paul, but I must get back. Susan will be wondering where I am.' She slammed the door behind her, and then wound down the window as the stifling atmosphere inside was airless. 'Goodbye.'

Paul stepped aside and raised one hand in salute, and with a feeling of escape she drove away. But the boy's face reflected in the rear-window was thoughtful, and she guessed, with a feeling of unease, that she had not seen the last of him.

Curiosity engulfed her as she drove along. He never mentioned his mother, or the possibility of his having brothers or sisters or both. The only person apart from his father she had heard him mention was his great-grandmother, and she must be very old. André's grandmother—she had to be eighty, at least, and yet she seemed an important person in the household. Of course, French households were not like English ones. In this country, the old were revered and respected, their opinions sought and valued, not ridiculed and dismissed as being of no account. Experience meant something here, and perhaps that accounted for Paul's obvious affection for his great-grandmother. But what about his mother? It should also be remembered that in this country, it was commonplace for a man to have a mistress. With painful insight Harriet had to admit she was curious. . .

There was no sign of Susan as she drove down the lane, and her nerve-ends tingled. She had been away only a little over an hour; surely nothing untoward could have happened in that time. And yet Susan invariably came out to meet her, and she obviously hadn't.

Stopping the car, she thrust open her door and got out, without bothering to collect her basket from the back seat. She walked quickly up the path and into the house calling: 'Susan! Susan, where are you?'

She had barely identified some horrifying spots on the stone flags of the kitchen floor as being blood when she heard a groan. It came from the *salon*, and she crossed the floor on unsteady legs, stifling her anxiety. In the doorway to the small parlour she halted, and then gasped in dismay. Susan was lying on the *chaise-longue*, her face as white as a sheet, while a seeping red stain from a carelessly-tied bandage below her knee was rapidly colouring the faded rose-pink velvet.

'*Susan!*' Harriet quelled the nausea that rose up inside her at the sight of so much blood. 'Oh, my God!'

Her legs felt weak and she grasped the doorpost to support herself. For a moment the room spun dizzily about her, as the effects of shock and too much sun combined to make her giddy.

'Harry—oh, Harry, I'm so glad you've come,'

Susan gulped and burst into tears. 'I've been so—so frightened!'

Harriet left the doorway to go across to her, comforting the girl as best she could while her eyes took in the possible extent of her injury. How had it happened? It seemed obvious that somehow Susan had gashed her leg. But when? And how deeply? And with what?

'Darling,' she exclaimed at last, when it seemed that Susan was going to cry for ever. The exertion was not good for her, and Harriet had to find out what she had done. 'Come on, love, tell me what happened.'

Susan gulped again and sniffed, and Harriet handed her a handkerchief to blow her nose, realising with an increasing sense of urgency that something had to be done, and quickly. Susan was losing far too much blood.

'It—it was the scythe,' Susan said at last, horrifyingly. 'I—I was trying to finish cutting the grass. You know—the grass that Paul left. . .'

Harriet could feel a sense of panic rising inside her. The scythe! Any accident was bad enough, and here they were, miles from a hospital, and no doctor that she knew of. Something had to be done, and fast, but what? Think, she told herself fiercely, *think!* Behave calmly! Don't let Susan see that you're going to pieces!

Pressing her trembling hands together, she knelt down on the floor and giving Susan what she hoped was an encouraging smile, she gently drew away the home-made bandage and exposed the wound. It was worse than anything she had imagined. A jagged gash revealed the whiteness of bone beneath tumescent, bloody flesh. Inches long, it obviously needed stitching, and the chances of infection from a garden implement were always present.

'I'm going to have to apply a tourniquet, Sue,' she said in a voice slightly higher than her normal one. 'We've got to stop the bleeding right now, and then we've got to see a doctor, right?'

She was trying to sound cheerful and competent, but she was aware that her words came out with little conviction. She was not naturally shocked by the sight of blood, but she had never had to deal with anything like this before, and even the idea of the tourniquet was gleaned from hearsay rather than actual experience in such a situation. They hadn't even got a medical cabinet at the house, and apart from aspirins she had nothing to relieve the pain the girl must be suffering.

'All right.' Susan was endearingly trusting, but Harriet felt sure her loyalty was misplaced. Here she was talking blandly—no, not blandly, blindly—about tourniquets and so on, but hadn't she also read somewhere that blood could only be cut off from part of the body for a certain length of time before gangrene set in? Gangrene! She shivered. If Susan lost a leg through this, she would always blame herself.

A pair of nylon tights provided an adequate

tourniquet and it was with some relief Harriet saw the flow of blood from the wound begin to ebb. But Susan was still terribly pale.

'I'm afraid I've spoiled your couch,' she said shakily, looking down at the stained velvet, but Harriet brushed her concern aside.

'The couch isn't important,' she assured her. 'You are. Now, we have to get you out to the car.'

'Where are we going?'

'To find a doctor,' said Harriet briskly, but the idea was a daunting one. And yet there had to be a doctor in Rochelac. There just had to be!

Susan was a weighty girl, however. In spite of the lack of flesh on her bones, she was too heavy for her aunt to carry, and after a few abortive attempts during which the leg was jarred several times, Harriet was weak and breathless, and Susan was obviously in pain.

'I—I'll have to walk,' she said, trying to be practical, but her face lost every scrap of animation as she attempted to get up from the couch.

'Stay where you are!' Harriet drew a deep breath as Susan turned anxious eyes up to her. 'I—I'll go and get somebody.'

Susan sank back against the cushions. 'Who?'

Harriet made a defeated gesture. 'Paul,' she said flatly.

CHAPTER SEVEN

THE journey to the chateau was a nightmare. Never having attempted it from the house before, she got caught up in thorns and creepers and had to retrace her steps to find the track beside the stream. It should have been easy, and perhaps if she had not been so desperate, it would have been. But it all took so much time, and the little knowledge she possessed was telling her she had none to lose.

She eventually reached the bridge that crossed the stream and from there the way was clear. She was hot and sweating, and her hands were scratched and grimy from fighting with the bushes, but she pushed back her hair and ploughed on, resisting the temptation to stop and dip her heated face in the cool water.

After another panting climb, she emerged on to the plateau beside the chateau walls. Of course, Paul was not about today, and quelling her nerves, she followed the path that ran round to the front of the building. Would Paul be home yet? It was almost an hour since she had left him in Rochelac, but would he go straight home, and if not, who else might she ask?

The tall gates of the chateau guarded their hollow monument with pride, and it was imposs-

ible not to admire the sun-bleached walls that
were topped by that magnificent parapet. But
her objective was the lodge whose outer wall
formed part of the surrounding fortifications of
the chateau, and her courage faltered as she saw
the studded door, and the bell-iron hanging
beside it. What would she say? How would she
introduce herself? Please, she prayed, please let
Paul be there!

The bell clanged forlornly through the stone
walls of the building, and she shifted restlessly,
waiting for someone to come and open the door
and relieve her of this almost painful anticipation. But the silence remained unbroken as the
sound of the bell died away, and she tugged it
again, growing impatient in her anxiety to get
back to Susan.

Again it seemed there was to be no reply, and
she was turning away, trying to suppress tears
of frustration when the sound of a key being
turned brought her to attention. She turned back,
throat dry and tight, as the heavy door swung
inward to reveal an elderly lady, leaning heavily
on a silver cane.

'Yes?'

She spoke in French, and Harriet gathered her
composure with difficulty. This had to be
Louise, she was thinking dazedly, realising for
all her frail appearance she was not as old as
she had estimated.

'I—' she began in English, and then switched
to French: 'I am sorry to trouble you, *madame*,

but I wanted to speak to—to your great-grandson, Paul.'

'Paul!' The old lady frowned. Piercing grey eyes incredibly like André's assessed her appearance without flinching. 'Why do you want to see my great-grandson, *mademoiselle?*'

'Oh, please, is he here?' cried Harriet desperately. 'My niece has had an accident. She's cut her leg, and I have to get her to a doctor. But I can't move her without assistance.'

'Ah.' The old lady nodded slowly. 'You must be Mademoiselle Ingram, no? You have bought the old farm.'

'Yes, yes. . .' Harriet had no time for polite conversation. 'Is Paul here?'

'No, he is not.' Harriet's hopes plummeted at her words. 'He is in Rochelac, *mademoiselle.*'

'Well. . .' Harriet pressed her lips tightly together. 'Is—is there anyone who could help me? His—his brother, perhaps. Or—or his mother?'

'Paul has no brothers, *mademoiselle.* Nor sisters either, I am sad to say. That young man would have more concern for his father if he had others to compete with. As it is—'

'I'm sorry, *madame,*' Harriet couldn't linger, 'but if there's no one here who can help me, I'll have to find someone who can—'

The old lady moved her head bird-like from side to side. 'Ay, ay, ay, you young people! You have no time to stand and talk to an old woman, I know.'

'It's not that,' Harriet stared at her helplessly. 'But my niece is alone. I must get assistance.'

'I am sorry, *mademoiselle*.' The old woman shook her head, and turning with careful movements, she closed the door in Harriet's face.

For a moment Harriet stared blankly at that closed door, and then she swung about and retraced her steps down the ravine. Her mouth was parched now, and she longed for a drink, but she had even less time to linger. As she walked, she gazed about her, wondering whether she was within hailing distance of anyone else, but the woods like the stream were solitary places, more used to birds and animals than human occupation.

At last she reached the lane and saw the house ahead of her. It looked so peaceful, dreaming in the noonday heat, but she paid little attention to its attractions. Somehow, between them, she and Susan would have to get her to the car. Once there, it would be a comparatively simple matter to get assistance. Perhaps now that she had had a rest, Susan would feel more up to it.

She entered the kitchen with some relief. She had left her dark glasses in the car, and it was a relief to feel her eyes shaded once more. Waiting a moment, to adjust her eyes to the light, she moved to the *salon* door, only to stop aghast when she saw her niece. Susan appeared to be unconscious. For some reason she had attempted to drag herself up from the couch, and in so doing loosened the tourniquet. She had collapsed on the floor, and now she lay there, blood seeping from her leg once more.

'Oh, God!' Harriet pressed her hands to her mouth. She couldn't move her alone. Unless she could manage to drag her to the car.

First things first, she told herself unsteadily, hurrying forward and dropping to her knees beside the helpless girl. In a moment she had tightened the tourniquet again, and then, when Susan made no move, she got to her feet and looked desperately down at her. She dared not leave her again and take the risk of Susan coming round and doing herself more injury. Somehow she would have to get the girl to the car alone, and perhaps it would be as well if she remained unconscious. What Harriet was planning to do was bound to hurt her.

A rug, that was what she needed, she decided positively. If she could shift Susan's weight on to a rug and drag her to the car that way, it might be easier all round.

Swinging about, she went back to the kitchen. The rugs she had bought for that room were too small, but upstairs, between the beds, was a sheepskin rug which might do.

She ran quickly up the stairs, ignoring her aching legs, rubbing the palms of her hands over the seat of her jeans to displace the moisture she could feel on them. Keep calm, she kept telling herself—but she wasn't altogether successful. Running down the stairs again, she almost fell, the ends of the rug trapping her toes, and the shock of it made her tremble.

'Careful!' she was chastising herself in an unsteady voice as she came into the kitchen, and then let out a choking gasp as a tall figure loomed suddenly in the open doorway. 'Oh, God! *André!*' she got out weakly, before collapsing in an untidy heap at the foot of the stairs.

He reached her in a moment, hauling her to her feet, and holding her between his hands until he had assured himself that she could stand alone.

'*Qu'est-ce que c'est?*' he demanded huskily, and she thought inconsequently how haggard he was looking. '*Qu'est-ce qui se passe?*'

'It's Susan!' she enunciated the words with difficulty, unable to coherently use his language. 'She—she's had an accident. With the scythe. I—I went to the chateau—'

'I know you did. How else do you think I am here?'

'Oh!' Harriet pushed back her hair with a distracted hand. 'Then your grandmother—'

'—told me only that you had given her some garbled story about needing Paul's assistance.'

Harriet gazed up at him. 'Paul—Paul said you wouldn't be there,' she stammered, and André gave a confused shake of his head.

'Paul *said?*' he echoed blankly. Then: 'Tell me later. Where is she?'

'Through here.'

Harriet led the way into the *salon*, and André brushed past her to kneel beside the unconscious

girl. He ran his thumbs over her eyelids, opening
the blank sockets with an expertise she knew
she would never possess, and then straightened,
taking in the blood-stained couch and Harriet's
amateur efforts at first aid.

'She's—she's lost a lot of blood, hasn't she?'
Harriet ventured unnecessarily, and he nodded.

'Yes.' He brushed past her again and went to
the sink in the kitchen to wash his hands. 'I will
take her to Charron in Bel-sur-Baux.'

'Charron?' Harriet followed him nervously.
'Is he a doctor?'

'He has a small clinic,' André agreed, drying
his hands again. 'Do you have something clean
with which we can bind the leg? And a blanket.
We do not want Susan to get a chill.'

'Oh, yes. Yes.' Harriet looked round abstractedly. Then: 'Are there no doctors in Rochelac?'

'None who can perform a transfusion,' he
replied patiently, going back to the *salon*. And
as she still lingered: 'A bandage, remember?'

Harriet hurried up the stairs. A clean pillowcase would have to do, and a blanket from the
foot of her bed. She came downstairs again to
find André had lifted Susan and was holding her
gently in his arms.

'Lay the blanket on the couch,' he instructed,
and she did so. He deposited the girl on the
blanket and then turned to take the pillowcase
from Harriet's nerveless fingers. 'Is this the
bandage?'

'It's all I've got,' she replied defensively,

and with a shrug, he tore it in half.

'You go ahead and open the door,' he advised, wrapping the cloth about Susan's leg as the girl began to stir.

'The door?' Harriet felt she was being absurdly stupid, but she couldn't help it. 'The door is open.'

'The door of my car,' he explained evenly, and she stared at him.

'I didn't know you came by car!'

'I do not suppose you were in any state to hear anything,' he retorted, and with a lingering glance at her niece, Harriet left the room.

The sunlight was blinding after the coolness inside, reminding her as it did how thirsty she still was. Parked along the lane, in front of the Fiat, was a dust-smeared station wagon, a Citroën, she surmised, which was badly in need of water, too. She walked quickly towards it, and swung open the rear door, looking round worriedly as she heard André call her name.

'Are you coming, too?' he demanded, and when she nodded, he added: 'Then had you not better lock your door?'

'Oh, yes.'

Harriet hurried back to the house, passing André and his burden on the way. Susan's eyes were open, and she looked anxiously at her aunt.

'It's all right, love,' Harriet whispered tenderly. 'You're going to be fine.'

'What happened?' asked Susan tearfully. 'Where are we going?'

'To see a doctor,' said André firmly, and looked pointedly at Harriet, who gulped and nodded, and ran quickly to lock the door.

When she came back André had installed Susan as comfortably as possible on the back seat of the station wagon. 'I think you had better sit up front,' he advised Harriet, as she would have got in the back beside Susan, and with a sympathetic smile at her niece, she did as she was asked.

André slammed his door and reversed expertly up the lane. The cushioned springing of the Citroën prevented Susan from being jarred too savagely, and then they were out on the road turning right towards Belsur-Baux. The signpost said seven kilometres, and Harriet felt a little of the tension of the past hour leave her. Less than five miles. That would not take long. And André knew where he was going. Even if she had got Susan to Rochelac, and to a doctor, it might have been a wasted effort.

She glanced sideways at the man whose lean brown hands were handling the wheel with firm assurance. She would have to thank him. It wasn't easy, feeling herself in his debt, but she was. He had handled Susan with such gentleness, and she felt a moment's anguish for the way she had treated him last time they met. And yet why should she? she justified herself defensively, staring blindly through the open window. He had brought her hatred upon himself, and goodness knows, she had enough to hate him for.

Susan stirred, and she seized the opportunity to break the awkward silence that had fallen between them. 'How do you feel?'

Susan's lips quivered. 'Shaky,' she admitted. 'And hot.'

She would have pushed the blanket aside, but André cast a look at her over his shoulder. 'Keep it on,' he said, and with a grimace she did as she was told.

'How did it happen?'

André's question was expected, and yet Harriet found it hard to answer him. 'Susan—I had gone into Rochelac and Susan decided to finish cutting the grass.'

'With the scythe?' André remarked grimly.

'Yes.' Harriet caught her lower lip between her teeth. 'Er—Paul was using it—before. I realise now I shouldn't have let him. It's a dangerous implement, I should have foreseen what might happen.'

She was burbling on, but she couldn't help it. The censure in André's expression was denigrating, and she felt stupidly incompetent. She couldn't help but imagine how she would have felt if Paul had had a similar accident, or worse, and delayed reaction was bringing a distinctly sick feeling to the pit of her stomach. It seemed hours since she had been sitting with Paul in the café in Rochelac drinking that coffee which now only accentuated the emptiness inside her.

'Are you feeling all right?'

André had apparently noticed her pallor, and

she shifted round in her seat so that he could not see her face. 'Yes,' she answered shortly. 'Yes, I'm fine.'

He made no further comment, speaking instead to Susan, assuring her that Docteur Charron was very kind and would soon have her feeling much more comfortable.

Bel-sur-Baux was a little bigger than Roch-elac, and set further down the valley. An arched bridge over a natural moat brought them into the busy square of the small town, where a stone fountain splashed water into a huge basin where children played. Natural stone buildings were bright with canopies of different colours, shading the lunchtime shoppers who thronged the busy parade, and balconies bright with pots of geranium and lobelia added their own brilliance to the scene.

André drove straight through the square, and into a narrow alleyway of cobbled stones. Iron stairways gave access to houses set above garages which had once been stabling for horses. As Harriet got out, conscious of the crumpled state of her denim shirt and jeans, she noticed the square plaque which advertised the Clinique Charron, and shifted uneasily as André lifted Susan out of the station wagon. Her legs felt numb and unwilling to do her bidding, but she forced herself to follow the others as André mounted the stairway to the white-painted door. It would be foolish if she broke down now, after the crisis was over. But she was glad of the handrail all the same.

A nurse-receptionist admitted them. She evidently knew André, which precipitated matters considerably. In next to no time, Doctor Charron was located, and Susan transferred to a stretcher-trolley and wheeled into the small operating theatre.

'Do you feel capable of giving them Susan's particulars?' André inquired, as they waited together in the anteroom, and Harriet drew an unsteady breath.

'I think so,' she answered. 'I—you needn't wait. This might take some time.'

André's mouth pulled down at the corners. 'You do not imagine she will be leaving here today, do you?' he demanded, and seeing her stunned expression added: 'They are bound to want to keep her under observation for at least twenty-four hours.'

'I—I never thought. . .' Harriet put a dazed hand to her head. 'You think she's going to be all right, don't you?'

'She has lost a lot of blood, but that is not an insurmountable barrier in this day and age, fortunately. The main danger is one of infection. I know Charron will make sure she has all the necessary injections.'

Harriet rubbed her hands together, and then looked down at them. 'Well, whatever—there's no need for you to waste any more time.'

André was silent for a moment, then he said

quietly: 'Did I say I was wasting time?'

'No, but—' She broke off awkwardly. 'You obviously are.' She pressed her palms together, avoiding the cool penetration of his eyes. 'I—I don't know how to thank you for helping us.'

'But it was not my help you sought, was it?' he reminded her bleakly. 'Perhaps you could tell me now how Paul came to be involved.' His thick lashes narrowed his eyes. 'Has he been troubling you again?'

'No.' Harriet shook her head. 'He—I—we met in Rochelac this morning. I—had coffee with him.'

'While Susan was cutting the grass?'

'I didn't know she was cutting the grass,' protested Harriet, sighing. 'And short of being downright rude to your son, I could hardly refuse his invitation.'

'Such consideration does not apply in my case, I take it,' he remarked dryly. 'You seem to have no such qualms where I am concerned.'

Harriet looked away from him. It was a small room, and he was too disturbing. Even in mud-stained levis and a rough cotton jacket, he had an overwhelming attraction for her, and the longer she was with him, the harder it became to put the memory of their last encounter out of her mind.

'I wonder how much longer they're going to be?' she murmured, anything to distract from the pregnant silence which had fallen, and he moved away to stand staring through the narrow panes of the window.

'Who gave you the idea to buy a house in the Dordogne?' he asked suddenly, and she thrust her hands into the pockets of her jeans so he should not see how they were shaking.

'I—well, I've always liked this area of France,' she replied jerkily. 'And Charles said houses were usually a good investment.'

'Charles,' he nodded.

'Yes, Charles Hockney—my employer.' She paused. 'I'm sure you remember him.'

She couldn't resist the barb, and he turned to look at her without liking. 'Oh, I remember Charles,' he agreed provokingly. 'And the horse-hair sofa he kept in his back room.'

Harriet's cheeks flamed. 'You would remember that of course!'

André's expression darkened. 'Why not? Why should I not remember it? We were happy there—once.

'You were,' she retorted, shortly, taking uneven steps about the room. 'Oh, I wish they'd let me know what's going on.'

André was looking at her and gathering her resources, she lifted her head and returned his stare. Why should he have it all his own way?

'You are telling me we were never happy together?' he demanded quietly, and her heart lurched.

'I'd really rather not talk about it,' she declared, beginning to feel the strain. 'Is—

is Doctor Charron a friend of yours?'

'You wish I should damn the good doctor to hell?' he extorted grimly. 'In the name of God, Harriet, speak to me as you do to my son! Tell me what it is I am supposed to have done!'

'You ask me that!' she gasped, and then dragged her gaze away from his. 'All right, *monsieur*—or should I say Comte?—tell me: how is your *wife?*'

His nostrils flared briefly, and then he bent his head. 'Did Paul not tell you his mother was dead?'

'*Dead!*' Harriet couldn't prevent the involuntary ejaculation. 'I—why, no! No, of course he didn't.' She raised both hands to the sides of her neck. 'Why didn't you tell me?'

'Would you have listened to me?' he enquired wryly. Then: 'She died six months ago.'

'Six months!' Harriet seemed unable to prevent herself from repeating everything he said. 'I'm—I'm sorry.'

'Are you?' His eyebrows lifted interrogatively. 'I do not see why. My wife was unknown to you.'

Harriet caught her breath. 'I'd feel the same if it was anybody. Death is always—painful.'

'It can be a release,' he retorted harshly. 'However, I accept the impersonality of your sympathy for what it is.'

Harriet glanced up at him uneasily. 'Did she—was she—had she been—ill?'

His lips thinned. 'Yes, she had been ill.'

'Was—was it a long illness?'

He expelled his breath on a sigh. 'A long illness, yes.'

'How long?' Suddenly it was imperative for her to know.

'Does it matter?'

'I'd like to know.'

He looked at her levelly. 'Ten—maybe eleven years.'

'Eleven years!' Harriet was horrified. That meant—that while she and André were seeing one another—The continuation of that train of thought was too awful to follow. Instead, she allowed her palms to cover her hot cheeks and moved away from him, putting the width of the small room between them.

'Another nail in my coffin?' he asked grimly. 'Yes, she was ill while I was seeing you. That is what you want to hear, is it not?'

'I don't *want* to hear it.'

'But it pleases you, does it not? It perhaps creates some justification for the way you are treating me, no?'

Harriet pressed her trembling lips together. 'It doesn't please me at all!' she retorted, but his lips had twisted scornfully.

'No? I get the distinct impression that you are searching for something to—how do you say it—feed the furnace of your hate! You do not like to feel indebted to me, and now you are happy.'

'That's not true!'

But he was turning away from her, wrenching open the door and walking out into the reception area, leaving her alone with the sickening knowledge that he was right. Despise him though she might, he was still the only man who could destroy every defence she raised against him.

She stepped to the door in time to hear him addressing the receptionist. He was asking what was going on, and she assured him smilingly that Docteur Charron would be ready for them very shortly. That the receptionist found André an attractive man was obvious, and when he smiled at her, Harriet felt her stomach muscles contracting painfully. She lay back against the wall beside the door, striving for control, but it was no use. Nausea overwhelmed her, and to her complete ignominy she retched and was unable to prevent the worst from happening.

She was aware of André and the receptionist appearing in the doorway, each registering expressions of concern. Then André's lean fingers closed round her arm, drawing her gently but firmly out of the now sour-smelling room and across the reception area to the outer door. The iron stairway outside was in shadow, and a slight breeze wafted coolly along the alley, fanning her scorched cheeks.

Harriet had never felt so humiliated. Pulling herself free of him, she leant her hands on the iron railing, gulping deeply of the fresh air, feeling the nausea subsiding.

Then she shuddered in remembrance. 'What

must she think of me?' she moaned, half to herself, but André heard her.

'Mademoiselle Dupois?' he murmured, resting back against the railing beside her. 'She is a nurse. She is used to sickness.'

Harriet cast him a sidelong look. 'I'm not the patient.' She lifted her shoulders awkwardly. 'I should have asked for the bathroom.'

André rubbed his nose reflectively. 'You did not appear to have had the time,' he remarked, and she looked at him quickly, half expecting he was mocking her, but he seemed perfectly serious as he added: 'Do you feel better now?'

Harriet still felt very unsteady. 'I—don't know,' she admitted honestly. 'It must be reaction from the shock.'

'Hmm.' He sounded sceptical. 'Have you had anything to eat today?'

'Um—some toast, this morning,' she told him.

'Is that all?'

'Well, it has been rather hectic, hasn't it?' she protested, and he straightened.

'Yes,' he nodded. 'In more ways than one, perhaps.' He opened the door for her. 'You may have your consultation with Charron and then we will have some lunch, yes?'

Harriet looked up at him. 'Why—why should you care whether—whether or not I have any lunch?' she faltered, and his mouth hardened.

'A good question,' he agreed equably, but he made no answer.

A junior nurse was mopping up the anteroom, and Harriet averted her eyes as she passed, her cheeks still burning with embarrassment. The receptionist was waiting, however, and came to speak to them.

'*Le médecin est prêt, maintenant!*' she said, smiling at Harriet. '*Avez-vous récupéré?*'

'I'm feeling much better, thank you,' Harriet answered in her language. 'I'm sorry for— well. . .'

'It is not important,' the girl reassured her easily. 'Please, follow me.'

André lounged into a seat in the reception area, and Harriet was forced to accompany the receptionist through swing doors that gave on to a corridor. The doctor's office was the second door along, and the receptionist left her here, no doubt eager to get back and talk to André, thought Harriet uncharitably.

Doctor Charron was younger than she had expected, a little above average height with pronounced side-burns and hair that was an indeterminate shade of brown. He was not a handsome man, but his white coat and air of authority gave him a certain attraction.

'Ah, Miss Ingram,' he greeted her in her own language, smiling slightly despite what Harriet felt must be her dishevelled appearance. 'Please sit down.'

Harriet subsided into the chair at the other side of his desk with some relief. She was still suffering the after-effects of the nausea, and anxiety about Susan and her condition was not conducive to relaxation.

Doctor Charron finished writing something in a folder, closed the file and then seated himself opposite her. '*Et maintenant*,' he said, folding his hands together where they rested on the desk. 'You are the aunt of the little one, *oui?*'

'*Oui*—I mean, yes.' Harriet pulled an apologetic face. 'How is she? Is she going to be all right? She lost such a lot of blood.'

Doctor Charron smiled reassuringly. 'I trust there is no need for concern, *mademoiselle*. The little one has lost a lot of blood, but that has been dealt with, and now we are left only with the possibility of infection.'

'Yes.' Harriet gripped the arms of the chair. 'Is it likely?'

He frowned and looked down at his hands. They were pale hands, smooth and well-manicured, not hard and calloused like André's, she thought treacherously, and then tried to concentrate on what the doctor was saying.

'I think we must keep your niece here, at least for tonight,' he said slowly. 'The leg itself must be rested, you understand, and we have all the facilities needed in case of any emergency.'

Harriet nodded. 'I see.'

He looked at her again, and his eyes were kind. 'I do not anticipate there being any emergency, Miss Ingram. Your niece is young and healthy. The cut was clean. Only the implement bothers me a little. Garden tools can be dangerous.'

Harriet nodded again. 'Can I see her?'

'But of course. First, however, perhaps you could give me some information about your niece—her name, date of birth, home address, and so on. It will not take a minute, and then you may visit for a short while. But—Susan, isn't it?' Harriet agreed, and he went on: 'Susan has been sedated, and I suggest you stay only a few minutes.'

Susan was drowsy when Harriet went in to see her, but she caught her aunt's hand in a rather anxious grip. 'You're not leaving me here, are you?' she cried.

'I have to,' said Harriet, squeezing her fingers comfortingly. 'It's only until tomorrow, and then we'll take you home.'

'But I don't speak French!' exclaimed Susan fretfully.

'They speak English,' Harriet said consolingly. 'You don't have to worry, darling. You'll be well looked after.'

'Where's Monsieur Laroche?'

Harriet stiffened. 'Why?'

'I'd like to see him, to thank him for bringing me here.'

'You can thank him tomorrow,' said Harriet firmly.

'You have to rest now. Recover your strength, so you can come home tomorrow.'

Susan looked a little tearful. 'Can't you come back later?'

Harriet hesitated. 'Perhaps I could. I'll ask as I go out. If I can, I will—I promise.'

Susan sniffed. 'They've stitched my leg. The nurse said there were twenty stitches.'

'Twenty!' Harriet shook her head. 'That's a lot.'

'I know.' Susan looked a little brighter at the realisation that she would have quite a story to tell her school friends when she got back to England. Then her mouth dropped again. 'I won't be able to play tennis again this year.'

'There's always next year,' said Harriet encouragingly, and then looked up as a nurse appeared. 'I think this means I have to go.'

S'il vous plaît,' said the nurse politely, and Harriet bent and kissed Susan's cheek.

'I'll see you later,' she whispered gently, and keeping a smile firmly in place, left the room.

But outside in the corridor, her confidence left her, and she walked towards the reception area feeling very much the alien in a foreign land. She supposed she would have to write to her mother and tell her what had happened, although she didn't look forward to that particular task. Mrs Ingram was inclined to fuss over the least thing, and a cut that needed twenty stitches was no minor injury.

The receptionist was at her desk as Harriet came through the swing doors, but there was no sign of André. To her disgust, her spirits sank even lower, but she put her own feelings aside and approached the desk.

'Will it be possible for me to come back later?' she asked, gesturing towards the wards. 'My niece is feeling rather low, and I wondered if I could visit her after—after—' she almost said *tea*, but changed it to: '—six.'

Mademoiselle Dupois looked thoughtful. 'I do not see why not,' she replied. 'But perhaps if you rang first. . .'

Harriet thanked her and moved away. She didn't feel disposed just then to explain that she did not have a phone, and besides, she would come back later, she decided. After all, she had nothing else to do. It was then she realised she had not brought her handbag with her, and aside from the fact that she had no means of transport, she had no money either. She faltered by the door, half inclined to ask the receptionist if she could lend her some money, when suddenly the door was propelled inward and André appeared. She was so relieved to see him, she stared at him speechlessly, and his mouth acquired a definite hardness.

'Is something wrong?' he exclaimed. 'Are you ready to go?'

'What?' Harriet gathered herself with difficulty. 'I—oh, yes. Yes.'

'Is Susan all right?' he demanded irritably, and she nodded.

'Like you said, they're keeping her in overnight.'

'*Bien*. So—shall we find somewhere to eat?'

Harriet dipped under his arm as he held the door wide for her, and stepped rather dazedly down the iron stairs. André joined her as they reached the bottom, and went ahead to swing open the door of the station wagon.

Harriet stopped beside the car, and aware of his continuing impatience with her, said: 'I—I thought you had gone,' in muffled jerky tones.

'Gone?' He stood holding the door, a blank expression on his face. 'Where would I go?'

'Why, home, I suppose. Back—back to the chateau.'

André pushed her rather roughly into the car, and then slamming the door walked round to get in beside her. He said nothing as he inserted the keys in the ignition and started the engine, and she pushed her hands together between her knees and wished she had never tried to explain.

They drove out of the alley, round the market square, and across the moated bridge out of the town. Harriet was surprised and disappointed. She had expected they would eat at one of the small cafés whose check-clothed tables looked so attractive in the sunlight, but evidently this was not to be. Perhaps André had thought better of his offer after she had behaved so stupidly, she thought, and a coldness invaded her stomach.

She was trying to summon up the courage to ask him where they were going, when he pulled off the road on to a leafy lane that seemed too narrow to lead anywhere. It ended abruptly in a barred gate, and beyond a lush meadow sloped down to the river, its banks a mass of buttercups and daisies. It was a beautiful spot, and the sound of a church bell in the distance tolling the hour only added to its charm.

André looked across at her then, noting her entranced gaze. 'I thought you would prefer this to eating in some café, under the eyes of a dozen people. You are a stranger here. People are curious.'

'We're having—a picnic?' she ventured, and he reached into the back of the station wagon and produced a long french loaf, some cheese, two velvety skinned peaches, and a bottle of wine.

'I got these while you were having your consultation with the good doctor,' he told her quietly, and she felt terrible.

'I didn't know—I never thought—' she faltered miserably, but he just gave a characteristic shrug of his shoulders and thrust open the car door. After a moment's hesitation Harriet joined him, and went quickly ahead to lift the iron hoop that held the gate in position.

The spreading branches of a chestnut tree provided an oasis of shade, and with Harriet's permission, André spread the blanket, which he had used to carry Susan, on the grass there. Harriet thought nothing had ever smelt so good as the bread when he broke it, releasing its warm fragrance into the air. She sat, legs drawn up, on the edge of the rug, gazing out across a scene which was at once familiar, yet unfamiliar. Its characteristics were the same as she might see at home, and yet she knew this could never be England. The colours were the same, but different. Greens were deeper, stronger, the purple line of the hills was harsher, and the heat haze that hung with lazy somnolence over the meadow had a not-unpleasant scent of herbs and wild garlic. A covey of wild geese, disturbed by some unseen intruder, surged up into the sky, their wings dark against the horizon, and Harriet rested her chin on her knees and wondered what unseen menace she was inviting.

CHAPTER EIGHT

ANDRÉ supported his back against the bole of the tree, and uncorked the wine with casual familiarity. 'I have no glasses, I regret,' he said, rubbing the neck of the bottle with the palm of his hand. 'Do you mind?'

Harriet shook her head, not trusting herself to speak and possibly spoil the beauty of the moment, and he handed the bottle to her so that she could drink first. It was still cool from the wine merchant's cellar and exquisitely refreshing; light and mild and only slightly dry, the taste lingered on her tongue long after she had handed the bottle back to him.

The bread tasted just as good as it smelled, and the cheese was strong and satisfying. A peach dripped syrup on to her fingers, and she licked at them child-like, her tongue darting provocatively out of her mouth. She found she was amazingly hungry considering the morning she had had, although she saw with some alarm that it was after three already.

'Won't—won't your grandmother wonder where you are?' she suggested tentatively, and André lowered the bottle he had just raised to his lips to look at her.

'Louise?' His eyes were disturbingly intent.

'Perhaps.' He lifted his shoulders in a dismissing gesture. 'No doubt she thinks I am back at work by now.'

Harriet rubbed the last drop of juice from her mouth with the back of her hand. 'You—work?' she probed daringly. 'What do you do?'

André rested his head back against the trunk of the tree.

'I am a farmer,' he told her flatly. 'What does a farmer do?'

Harriet's eyes widened. 'But. . .' She hesitated, and then plunged on: 'You are the Comte de Rochefort!'

André's lips curled. 'I am André Laroche,' he corrected her harshly. 'What use are empty titles to me?'

Harriet assumed a studied concentration of her toes. She knew his situation was not unique. All over Europe, standards were changing. In England, many of the large estates had had to be sold or given over to the National Trust, and wealth was no longer an accepted heritage. But this was more personal somehow.

'What is the matter?' he asked her suddenly. 'It is an honest way to earn one's living, is it not?'

'Oh, yes.' Harriet was quick to agree with him.

'Then why do you look so—subdued?'

Harriet made a helpless movement of her shoulders. How could she explain that this new image of him did not fit in at all with the image she had kept over the years: of a man who avoided telling her his occupation, because he didn't have one? And besides, she knew his hands had not been so rough eight years ago as they were now.

'I—I suppose I'm sorry that you cannot maintain the chateau now as you used to do,' she murmured awkwardly, and sensed his disbelief.

'Perhaps you consider a poor farmer is not good enough to share his lunch with you,' André suggested grimly, and she turned hurt eyes in his direction.

'That's not true!' she declared, shaking her head indignantly. 'If you must know, it just didn't—fit in with what I knew of you.'

'What you think you know of me,' he amended caustically, and then he uttered an angry imprecation. 'Oh, forget it! It is too hot an afternoon to argue.'

He closed his eyes against her, and she found herself clenching her fists tightly. He had taken off his cotton jacket, and unbuttoned the shirt beneath almost to his waist, and her eyes lingered on the sweat-moistened expanse of his chest. His legs were stretched out lazily in front of him, and the strong muscles of his thighs were outlined against the taut cloth. She found herself wondering what his wife had been like, and whether he had loved her very much. They had only had one child, but that could mean anything. Paul's mother might have had a difficult pregnancy—there could have been compli-

cations afterwards. Or perhaps she hadn't
wanted any more children. *Had he*? Harriet's
hand sought the flatness of her own stomach,
and a shudder ran through her. Would it have
made any difference if he had known?

She was still looking at him when his eyes
opened again, and immediately she looked away.
But not before their eyes had met, and she had
seen the deepening interest in his. To distract
his attention, she began gathering the remains
of the picnic together, pushing rind and peachs-
tones into a paper bag, rescuing the cork and
looking about for the bottle. Then she saw it was
still in his hand, and that it was not yet empty.

'Are you thirsty?' he enquired, but she shook
her head.

'No, I—I just wondered where the bottle was,
that's all,' she explained uncomfortably. 'I'm
sorry if I disturbed you.'

'You always disturbed me,' he said, and her
pulses raced madly.

He moved away from the tree and stretched
his length beside her on the blanket. For a
moment, she thought he was going to touch her
and every nerve in her body grew taut with
anticipation. But he didn't. He merely flexed his
muscles and stretched his legs, then raised the
wine bottle to his lips to take another drink.

She wanted to move away from him. His arm
was only inches from her thigh, but to do so
would seem so obvious somehow. Besides, she
should be capable of sitting beside him without

feeling this supreme awareness of him.

'Tell me something,' he said suddenly, 'why have you never got married?'

Harriet stiffened. 'Nobody asked me.'

'Now I find that hard to believe,' he said, his eyes half closed. 'What about all those eager young men you knew in your home town?'

'I moved from Guildford,' she said shortly. 'I live in London now.'

'*Eh bien*, are there not men in London?' He flicked a dark glance at her. 'I do not believe you do not have admirers.'

Harriet's throat felt tight. 'After you, you mean?' she got out chokingly. 'Do you think because I slept with you, I would do the same with any man?'

André swore violently and rolled on to his side facing her. 'No,' he denied gratingly, 'I do not think any such thing. But I am not a fool, I hope. I have disciplined myself to accept that I should not be the only man to arouse you in that way!'

'So you think I've had affairs, is that it?' Her tone was bitter. 'Well, perhaps I have. You'll never know, will you?'

'*Harriet*!'

The way he said her name caused an unwilling thrill of excitement to surge along her veins, and when he said it again, more emotively this time, her whole body ached to respond to the urgency in his voice.

'Harriet,' he groaned protestingly, running his

fingers the length of her thigh. 'You have no idea what you are doing to me. . .'

Her denim jeans covered her legs, but that didn't stop the caress of his fingers from burning the skin beneath. Her whole body seemed consumed by fire, and she took huge breaths of air, trying to keep her sanity. But all that happened was that she drew his attention to the swelling roundness of her breasts, and he jack-knifed into a sitting position and slowly but systematically unfastened every button on her shirt.

'Please. . .don't!' she begged, trying to cover herself, hot with embarrassment, but he just pushed her hands away, and bending his head to the burgeoning fullness, murmured:

'Do not be ashamed. You are beautiful. . . beautiful.'

'André. . .'

Her hands clenched in her lap, but her objections went unanswered. He seemed drugged by the sensuous warmth of her body, and it was useless to deny that she wanted him to touch her. He pushed the offending shirt down over her arms, and caressed the soft skin of her shoulders. And then he lowered her back against the blanket and parted her lips.

His mouth was an insistent assault on her senses. She could feel his weight upon her, and the roughness of his body hair against her breasts, but she refused to respond to him. She kept her eyes open and gazed up at that unchanging arc of blue overhead, and remembered what could happen if she gave in.

He sensed her detachment, of course, although she couldn't prevent the physical effects his stimulus had on her. It was becoming increasingly difficult to remain immune, and her hands yearned to stroke the smooth skin of his back, to touch his hips and mould herself even closer.

Then, with a muffled oath, he rolled away from her to lie on his back beside her with both hands pressing on the top of his head as if somehow to prevent it from bursting.

He drew a short uneven breath, and said roughly: '*Enfin*, it is finished!' and got savagely to his feet. He reached for his jacket with hands that were not quite steady, adding: 'Come: we will go.'

Harriet hadn't realised she had been holding her breath until she began to move, and then it was hard to drag oxygen into lungs that were tortured with the same tightness that gripped her throat. What was the matter with her? she asked herself despairingly, sitting up and groping for her shirt, pulling it over her shoulders again. She had made him see that she was no longer the impressionable girl she had been, that he could not fool her a second time. So why didn't she feel at peace with her victory?

When she got to her feet, André picked up the blanket and the bag containing their litter. Harriet reached for the wine bottle lying forlornly on the grass, and saw that the wine that had been left had all run away into the soil.

What a waste, she thought wretchedly, following André to the gate, but it was a reflection of their relationship too, and she had to fight back the tears that threatened to overwhelm her.

It took little time to reverse back up the lane, and cover the remaining kilometres to the house, but when they got there André, who had been silent throughout the journey, spoke:

'Will you go back to Bel-sur-Baux in the morning?'

Harriet was preparing to get out of the station wagon, but she paused and glanced swiftly at him. 'As—as a matter of fact, I've promised to go back this evening,' she admitted reluctantly. 'Susan was not too happy when I left her, so I said I would try and see her again later today.'

'I see.' André's brows lowered. 'Do you think that is wise?'

'Why not?'

She was quick to argue with him, but he spread his palms in a gesture of acquiescence. 'As you will,' he essayed quietly, and when he said no more she had, perforce, to get out of the vehicle.

'I—thank you again,' she murmured awkwardly, but he just shook his head and reversed smoothly away.

The house was depressingly empty. Harriet wandered through the quiet rooms, suppressing the urge to give in to self-pity, and determinedly got herself a bucket of cold water and some clean cloths to sponge the blood-stained *chaise-*

longue. But as she worked with her hands, her mind was free to wander at will, and inevitably she thought about what André had told her of his wife.

She wondered what manner of illness it could have been to last so many years. There were various alternatives, and she guessed how destructive such an illness could be to a marriage. But that was no excuse for André's behaviour, she told herself vehemently, rubbing harder than was necessary and making her arm ache. Just because his wife was ill, an invalid maybe, it did not give him the right to find diversion elsewhere. But again, it was a common enough situation here, and perhaps his wife had condoned his behaviour.

But no, that would not do. Harriet rested back on her heels. Reading her thoughts, anyone would think she was trying to excuse him; or was she only trying to excuse herself? And for what? What had she done to feel so out of countenance with herself? The answer was unacceptable to her.

She forced herself to eat an omelette before setting out for the hospital once more. This time she went in her car and took her handbag, deliberately wearing a dress of clinging silk jersey, whose apricot folds flared below her hips and accentuated the slender length of her legs. She wanted Mademoiselle Dupois to see that she did not always look like a dishevelled teenager and was disappointed to find the young receptionist was no longer on duty. Instead, an elderly woman occupied the chair behind the reception desk, and she looked doubtfully at Harriet when she asked to see her niece.

Speaking in French, she asked whether Harriet had Doctor Charron's permission to see his patient, and when Harriet admitted she hadn't, she gave an apologetic little shake of her head.

'I regret the doctor has been called away on another case,' she explained, 'and I cannot sanction your visit without his permission.'

Harriet sighed. 'But my niece only cut her leg,' she protested. 'You're only keeping her in overnight.'

'I am sorry.' The woman was shaking her head again when a door opened behind them, and a draught of cool air signified someone's arrival. Harriet swung round, and then felt instinctively relieved when she saw Doctor Charron. The doctor was not wearing his white coat this evening, but his air of authority remained, and after a moment's hesitation he came towards Harriet with his hand oustretched.

'Miss Ingram!' he exclaimed. 'I—how nice to see you again. Have you come to see your niece?'

Harriet guessed he hardly recognised her as the harassed individual he had interviewed this afternoon, but he hid his astonishment very well.

'I wondered if I might,' Harriet said now, allowing him to take her hand. 'If you are agreeable.'

'I have no objections, *mademoiselle*,' he assured her, 'but I am afraid you may find she is asleep. She was awake earlier, when your friend was here, but now—'

'My friend?'

Harriet gazed at him blankly, and the doctor nodded. 'Of course. Laroche—the Comte de Rochefort. He is a friend of yours, is he not?'

Harriet's fingers tightened round her handbag. 'He came back?'

'While Susan was having supper, yes. She seemed very pleased to see him.' He paused. 'Of course, as her guardian you must tell me if I was wrong to permit him to visit with her.'

'Oh, no—no!' Harriet shook her head agitatedly. But she was disturbed by what she had heard. And yet why? Why shouldn't André visit Susan if he wanted to? Obviously, Susan herself had no objections, so why should she?

'Come.' The man seemed to sense her distress. 'We will go and see if she is awake.'

But Susan was asleep, breathing soundly, her colour good and a faint smile curving her lips. Doctor Charron laid his fingers against the side of her neck and studied his watch for a moment. Then he shrugged and came back to where Harriet was standing at the foot of the bed.

'She is making good progress,' he said softly, so as not to disturb the girl. 'If her leg shows no sign of septicaemia in the morning, I think we can let her go. But you must promise to bring her back at once if any discoloration takes place.'

'Of course.'

Harriet nodded, and at his indication preceded him into the corridor again. As they walked towards reception, however, Doctor Charron made another suggestion.

'It seems a pity,' he said, 'that you have made the journey for nothing. With your permission, perhaps we might have dinner together.'

Harriet looked sideways at him. His face was perfectly serious, a certain expectancy deepening the blue of his eyes. 'I'm sure you must have work to do, doctor,' she said, not wanting to let him down too heavily, but he shook his head.

'I merely came back to the clinic to check with Nurse Gaston that there had been no emergency,' he explained. 'As there obviously has not, I am free for the remainder of the evening.' He paused, watching the play of emotions across her expressive face. 'Please. I would be honoured if you would join me.'

Harriet still hesitated. She liked Doctor Charron. She thought he was a kind and intelligent man. But she was loath to get involved with any man, least of all one who knew André.

'I don't know. . .' she murmured, as he held the swing door wide for her to pass through. 'I'm not awfully hungry.'

He smiled, and she thought how much younger he looked when he did so. 'Then come and watch me eat,' he adjured her humorously, and with a laugh she gave in.

'All right,' she agreed, mentally assuring herself that there was no earthly reason why she shouldn't accept his invitation. He was an attractive man, and besides, the empty house held little appeal right now. Perhaps an evening with someone objective, someone who knew nothing about her, would help to lift the veil of despondency which seemed to have enveloped her.

They dined at a restaurant overlooking the square. The fountain was floodlit at night, and the water glittered with shifting colours. Although the restaurant was small, the food was superb, and Harriet found herself accepting some of the truffle-flavoured pâté for which the area was famous, and following it by a little chicken lightly cooked in cream and brandy.

'I really didn't think I was hungry, Doctor Charron,' she confessed a little later, raising her wine glass to her lips, and smiling at him across the lighted candle in the centre of the table.

'I guessed you might not be able to resist Henri's cuisine,' Charron said, matching her action. 'And my name is Marcel. I would like you to use it.'

'Marcel.' Harriet said the word experimentally. Then she put her glass down. 'You know mine.'

'Harriet.' He nodded. 'I have never known anyone called Harriet before.'

He said her name as André did, without the benefit of an *h*, and for a moment it gave her a pang. She wondered what André was doing this evening, whether he had told his grandmother—

and incidentally, his son—about Susan's accident. She had learned a lot about him today, but there was still so much she didn't know, would never know. . .

Marcel was an entertaining companion, and in spite of herself Harriet enjoyed the evening. She told him of her work, and her interest in ceramics, and he insisted she must see the porcelain and enamel works at Limoges. She agreed that Limoges was worth a visit, but that she had already been there with Charles a couple of years before. It was then that she had become attracted to the area, and when only recently Charles had suggested she might buy a property there, she had been more than interested.

As she had come to Bel-sur-Baux in her own car, Marcel was denied the opportunity of driving her home, and she was half relieved. He was a nice man, and she had enjoyed his company throughout the evening, but she did not want to have to fend off advances at this stage of their relationship.

'I will see you tomorrow then,' he said as he escorted her to where she had parked the Fiat, just off the market square. 'You are sure you know your way home?'

'I'm sure.' Harriet opened the door and got inside before he could make any move to touch her. 'And thank you again for a lovely evening.'

'It was my pleasure,' he assured her gallantly, and stood back with his hand raised as she drove away.

It was dark now, and the road was twisting and unfamiliar. Harriet wondered if she had been over-confident in saying she knew the way home, and then breathed a sigh of relief when the signposts appeared on her right and she saw the turning into the lane. She took the car out of gear and let it cruise comfortably down to the house, and then had to step on her brakes as the outline of another vehicle suddenly loomed ahead of her. It was André's Citroën, and her heart skipped a beat as she turned off the engine and stepped out of her car.

She glanced apprehensively towards the house, but there were no lights, and then she started violently as the station wagon's door was pushed open, and André himself got out. She could just make out his profile in the light that briefly appeared as he opened the door, but then he closed it again and the illumination was quickly extinguished.

'What are you doing here?' she burst out impulsively, aware of a ridiculous feeling of guilt at the remembrance of how she had spent her evening, but he strolled indolently towards the gate and said:

'Shall we go inside?' without answering her.

She was tempted to argue, but common sense warned her not to provoke him, and with an impatient shrug she went through the gate he had opened for her, and up the path.

Once the door was open, André went ahead and lit the lamp while Harriet drew the flowered yellow curtains across the windows. Then she turned to face him, conscious of her appearance and what interpretation he might put on it. This evening he was more formally attired in black suede pants and a matching silk shirt, the dark colours accentuating his evidently sombre mood. He took up a position before the empty grate, and said quietly: 'You have been to the hospital?'

'Yes.' At least she could be truthful. 'So have you.'

He inclined his head. 'Susan told you?'

'No.' She hesitated. 'Er—Doctor Charron did.'

'You saw Charron?' André acknowledged this thoughtfully. 'And what did he say?'

Harriet licked her dry lips. 'He—he said she seems to be making good progress.' Another pause, then: 'Susan was asleep.'

André's eyes narrowed. '*Vraiment*?' She noticed again how in moments of unconscious stress he used his own language. But he quickly recovered himself again. 'You have been waiting for her to wake up?'

'No. I. . .' Harriet was finding this increasingly difficult, and she was angry with herself that this should be so. After all, it was nothing to do with him how she spent her time. 'As a matter of fact, I had dinner with—Doctor Charron.'

It was out, and she saw the gaunt tightening of the skin over his cheekbones. '*Vraiment*, is that so?'

Harriet adopted a defensive air. 'You don't object, do you? I am a free woman, you know. I can choose how—and with whom—I spend my evenings.'

He surveyed her coldly. 'Did I suggest otherwise?'

'No, but—oh, well, it doesn't matter.' She shook her head frustratedly, her heavy hair swinging about her shoulders. 'You haven't told me why you're here yet.'

He put his hands behind his back, the action straining the buttons of his shirt so they gaped across his chest. 'I came, on Louise's instructions, to ask whether you would care to join us for supper,' he told her, and she felt a wave of shame sweep over her. '*Evidemment*, it is too late now,' he continued bleakly, 'but I became concerned when you did not return from the clinic, and decided to wait for you.'

'Oh!' Harriet expelled her breath jerkily. 'I see.' She put down her handbag on the table, avoiding his eyes. 'I'm sorry.'

'*N'importe*!' He shook his head. 'You are here now.'

But it did matter. Harriet was very much aware of her own behaviour, and as always with him she felt the offender. 'Please,' she said awkwardly, 'thank your grandmother very much for her invitation. I—maybe I could accept some other time.'

André regarded her sceptically. '*Peut-être*. Paul said you would not come to my house.'

Harriet's face flamed. 'That was different. That was before—before—'

'—before you knew my wife was dead?' André's eyebrows lifted.

Harriet moved her shoulders. 'Perhaps.'

André's expression hardened. 'I should not have thought that would make any difference to you.'

Harriet gasped. 'Well, you were wrong!'

'Was I?' His nostrils flared, and she could see he was holding his temper in check by a supreme effort of will power, 'And yet this afternoon, you rejected me with every fibre of your being!'

Harriet was glad of the table between them, glad of its support. 'I think you had better go,' she declared tremulously. 'I—am rather tired.'

His hands came to his sides, the knuckles taut, and Harriet made a final effort to behave naturally. 'Thank you—thank you again for what you did today.'

He made an indifferent gesture. 'I would have done the same for anyone,' he told her callously, and she winced. '*A propos*, there is one thing more.' He paused, and her nerves tightened at the chilling bitterness in his eyes: 'You must get the good doctor to introduce you to *his* wife some time.'

Harriet felt all the colour draining out of her face. 'He's. . .married. . .?' she breathed.

'For a great number of years,' André agreed scornfully. 'How unfortunate you are in your choice of escorts!'

Harriet's lips trembled. 'You—you swine! You enjoyed telling me that, didn't you?' she accused recklessly. 'What pleasure you must get out of seeing me squirm!'

Now it was André's turn to look discomfited. 'Do not be foolish!' he retorted. 'Would you rather I had left you in ignorance? What would you do if Madame Charron came to your door, as she has gone to others in the past, and accused you of being—*bien*, in polite terms, a loose female.'

'Woman,' amended Harriet automatically, dragging her eyes away from his contemptuous face. 'I only have your word that she might.'

'And of course my word is not good enough, is it?' he suggested harshly, but she made no response. 'So—' He looked towards the door. 'You will be all right here, will you not?'

'Don't pretend it matters to you!'

'You know it does,' he retorted coldly, and her breathing quickened. 'Everything you do matters to me, but that is something I have learned to live with.'

Harriet's lips parted. 'Please. . .' she got out chokingly, 'don't say such things to me! We both know they're not true, and I'm not about to make the same mistakes again.'

André made a defeated gesture. 'You are so hard, Harriet. But perhaps you are right. Perhaps it is already too late.' He sighed. 'I did not believe it, but. . .' He shook his head expressively.

Harriet turned tortured eyes in his direction. 'What do you want from me, André? What do you want me to say? That I've forgiven you? That I've forgotten the cavalier way you treated me?'

'Cavalier?' he echoed roughly. 'What is this? I am no cavalier.'

'No, you're not,' she flared unsteadily. 'Anything but!'

'Then why do you say it?'

'Oh—' She dismissed the word with a wave of her hand. 'It means—carelessly, thoughtlessly. I think you know what it means.'

'I think you exaggerate,' he told her grimly. '*Très bien*, I accept that my allowing you to come to Paris damns me in your eyes, but I have to remind you that you wanted to come—I might even say *begged* to come!'

'Oh, that's beautiful, isn't it?' Harriet gazed bitterly at him. 'Shifting the blame on to me!'

'Blame?' He looked heavenward for a moment as if for inspiration, and then came purposefully towards her, ignoring her protests and grasping her firmly by the shoulders. 'Why in the name of God should I feel any blame?'

He was too close and she was too disturbed. His nearness suffocated her. It had been a long day and she made tiredness the excuse for the weakening she felt towards him. His fingers were biting into her shoulders, but she was glad of their support, dependent as she was on legs that threatened to give out on her. Her eyes were on a level with the base of his throat where the open neck of his shirt revealed the pulse that was beating there, rapidly increasing as he continued to hold her.

That small palpitation was mesmerising. An intense desire to give in to him was rising treacherously inside her, and she found herself fighting for control. But what sweet revenge it would be if she could respond to him, break down his guard, and then spurn him at the moment when he thought she was his.

It was like contemplating playing with fire. And was that really what she wanted? Or was she only seeking excuses to let him make love to her because it was becoming an obsession with her? Somehow, she had to destroy this weakness, and there was only one way she knew.

'How do you think I felt when I got your letter?' she demanded tremulously, forcing herself to meet his gaze. 'You must have known I had no idea.'

André's lips tightened. 'How do you think I felt writing it?' he parried. 'It was not easy, believe me.'

'Why did you do it?' she cried desperately, and his eyes narrowed.

'Do you mean—write the letter?' He shook his head wearily. 'No, I thought not. So—why did I let you come to Paris?'

'Why did you make me fall in love with you!' she choked.

His eyes darkened. 'It was a mutual thing.

And I had no control over it.'

'You should never have spoken to us at the salerooms!'

'And you should have taken Charles' advice, no?' He shook his head again. 'Harriet, I did try. I stopped seeing you. But you wanted to see me! And God forgive me, I could not refuse you.'

Harriet pulled herself away from him. 'What—what did you think happened, after— after you wrote that letter?'

He heaved a sigh. 'I tried not to think. I tried not to imagine you with some other man, sharing with him the intimacies you had shared with me!'

His voice was hoarse, and she turned anxious eyes on him. 'But didn't you—didn't it occur to you to wonder whether—' She broke off and looking away from him tried again. 'Didn't you ever think that there might be some—some payment demanded for that night we spent together?'

'*What*!' She had his undivided attention now as he swung her round to face him, eyes glittering, his hand curled round the flesh of her upper arm. 'What are you saying?'

She trembled. 'What—what do you think I am saying?'

'You are telling me that you were—*pregnant*?' He stared disbelievingly at her, and then seeing the anguish in her face added more gently: 'You were pregnant!'

She held up her head, half regretting the impulse to tell him. 'Maybe.'

'*Harriet*!' His tone was harsh now. '*Nom de dieu*, tell me the truth, for pity's sake!'

'All right, all right.' She spoke unsteadily, trying to prise his fingers from her arm. 'I'll tell you. Yes. Yes, I was pregnant!'

'*Non*!' He said the word without conviction. '*Oh, non*!'

His hand fell from her arm and he put both hands to his face, pressing back the skin of his cheeks for a moment, before sliding distractedly through his hair.

Then his hands dropped to his sides again, and her heart ached for the torment he was suffering. 'The child,' he said hoarsely. 'Where is the child?'

Harriet bent her head. 'It's dead,' she said, unable to keep the tremor from her voice. 'It was born dead. I—I had to keep working to support myself, and I fell from some steps only weeks before it was due to be born.' She swallowed the lump that had come into her throat. 'It—it was a girl. A—perfect little girl!'

Her voice broke then, and with a groan André reached for her, and this time she made no protest. He enfolded her in his arms, and she pressed her face between the opened vee of his shirt, and wept into the cloud of dark hair that filled her nose and mouth.

Eventually her sobs subsided, but she did not draw away, and he made no effort to let her go.

On the contrary, if anything he held her closer, moulding her yielding body to his, making her insistently aware of what holding her like this was doing to him.

She knew she ought to pull away from him. Just because she had told him now it did not change the situation. His culpability did not end with confession, and his sympathy and compassion were not what she wanted.

But there was something so good about being close to him like this, and her lips moved against his chest almost of their own volition. A shudder ran through him and she felt his hand slide up to her nape, turning her face up to his. His eyes were dark pools in which she would willingly have drowned herself, his mouth twisting sensuously as he saw the tender vulnerability of hers. The pulse at his throat was beating erratically now, physical evidence of his throbbing emotions, arousing her response to his virile masculinity.

'Harriet?' he whispered hoarsely. 'Do not send me away. . .'

Her whole body seemed to be consumed by fire, and there was little she could do against the tide of feeling which was sweeping away all lingering remnants of common sense. This was André, her senses told her, the man she had never forgotten, the man to whom she had given everything, including her heart. . . The scent of him was all about her, clean and masculine, melting her resistance, filling her with the knowledge of her need of him, fulfilling the reasons for her existence.

With a little moan, she surrendered to him, winding her arms about his neck, pressing her firm breasts against him, opening her mouth eagerly beneath the hard pressure of his. A kind of madness was possessing her, and when his lips left her mouth to seek the creamy skin rising from the unbuttoned neckline of her dress, she encircled his neck with her fingers, pressing his head closer to the scented hollow he sought, arching her body sinuously to the thinly restrained urgency of his.

'Harriet. . . Harriet. . .' he groaned, his hand probing the neckline of her dress, sliding under the revealing material to find the taut nipple outlined against the cloth. His fingers were hard, but caressing, arousing her to the realisation that she wanted him to lose what little control he had. The house was so quiet, they were alone here, they could have been the only human beings left alive in the world for all she cared at that moment, and soon she knew there would be no turning back. . .

'*Mon dieu!*'

The anguished exclamation was as damning as it was unexpected. To Harriet it was like a douche of cold water, but for André it was something worse. Paul stood transfixed in the open doorway, staring at them as if he had never seen either of them before. Then with a coarse epithet he turned away, and they heard him go threshing off into the darkness.

Harriet felt sick. André had had to let her go when his son appeared, and now she dragged the bodice of her dress closely about her, feeling very much the 'loose female' Madame Charron might have accused her of being.

'Harriet!' André turned to her desperately, his face haggard with emotion. 'Harriet, I have to go after him.'

'Of course.'

Her tone was expressionless, she was concentrating on the floor at her feet, and he stared at her frustratedly. 'Harriet, do not let this come between us. . .'

'Between us?' She lifted her head. 'What is there between us, André, except sex—and good old-fashioned lust?'

'That is not true!' He turned to stare out into the darkness, and then looked at her again. 'Harriet, please—let me come back—'

'No.'

'*Que veux-tu dire, non?*'

'I mean no. N. O. Negative. Oh, go away, André. Go and find your son. Can't you see I just want to be left alone?'

'You are overwrought—'

'No,' she corrected him. 'I *was*, but now I'm sane again. You can thank Paul for me. Without his intervention, I might have lost all self-respect!'

André's shoulders sagged. He looked unutterably weary, and just for a moment her emotions stirred. But then she remembered his wife, and how she must have felt, knowing her husband had a mistress. Nothing could alter what had gone before. It would always be there between them. And if she couldn't trust him then, why should she trust him now?

CHAPTER NINE

'BUT why do we have to go back to England?' Susan protested disappointedly. 'Oh, I know my leg needs time to heal, but couldn't it heal just as well at Rochelac?'

Harriet concentrated on negotiating the road junction and cursed silently as she jarred her gears. 'Susan, Doctor Charron admitted that regular bathing was essential, and I dread to think what he would say if he knew we mostly used the stream, or that primitive iron bath I found in the shed!'

'But the bath is clean. I could use that.'

'Every day? Who's going to carry all the water?' Harriet glanced sideways at her. 'Be sensible, Susan. It just isn't on.'

'But you said nothing about this yesterday,' Susan objected, and her aunt sighed.

'Yesterday neither of us was thinking very sensibly,' she averred firmly. 'I—well, I've had time to think now, and although I'm as sorry as you are'—she surreptitiously crossed her fingers at this point—'there doesn't appear to be any alternative.'

Susan sniffed. 'You mean Gran's, don't you?' she mumbled, near to tears now. 'Or have you forgotten I haven't got a home?'

'Oh, Sue!' Harriet felt horribly mean. 'No, you don't have to go to Gran's, if you don't want to. You can stay at the flat, with me. At least, until it's time for you to go back to school.'

'Can I? Can I really?' Susan brightened considerably. 'Oh, I wouldn't mind that. I mean, there's lots more to do in London, isn't there? And perhaps, as I'm only going to be able to limp around for a while, that would be easier.'

'Hmm.'

Harriet forced a smile, trying not to consider what going back to London would mean to her. She had hardly slept a wink the night before, and this morning she had felt like death. But a blusher and some cleverly applied cosmetics had erased much of her pallor, and only her eyes revealed the tortuous agony of her thoughts.

And yet she knew that what she was doing was for the best. She had lived eight years without André; she would learn to live without him again in time. Perhaps he had cared about her in his own way, and no doubt he did regret what had happened. But there were some things that not even time could amend, and it was better to make a clean break than to allow the situation to drag on to its ultimate conclusion.

Susan's accident might have been for the best, after all. At least it gave her a satisfactory reason for leaving, and she would contact the agent once she got back to England and have him sell the property. She would be sad to see it go, in spite of everything. She had grown fond of its uneven floors and rough-washed walls, and the fragrant smell of wild lavender that pervaded the once-derelict rooms.

She deliberately cast her thoughts forward to England, to London, and to Charles. No doubt he would be surprised to have her back after only a month, but she wanted to get back to work, to occupy her mind as well as her hands.

'When do you think we'll be leaving?' Susan asked, after her aunt had got her comfortably ensconced on the *chaise-longue* just outside the door of the house. She looked up at the bright sunlight. 'Won't you be sorry to leave all this?'

'I expect I'll soon find something else,' Harriet assured her briefly. Then: 'Now, will you be all right if I go and start packing?'

'You didn't tell me when we were leaving!' Susan protested, and her aunt sighed.

'I don't know. Tomorrow, or the next day, I expect. I have to let Doctor Charron know. He'll give me all your papers to hand on to our own doctor.'

Susan pulled a face. 'I wish we didn't have to go. Couldn't you change your mind, Harry?'

'No.'

Harriet was firm, and with a little hunching of her shoulders, Susan turned her back on her.

All day Harriet expected André to appear, but he didn't, and she went to bed that night with the discomfiting realisation that she was disappointed. Oh, God, she thought, banging her pillow into shape, what did she want, after all?

She had told him to go, not once but several times, and if he had chosen to take her literally at last, why should she complain?

But she would have liked to see him one last time, she thought forlornly, just to tell him she was leaving, to say goodbye. It would have tied the ends up, somehow.

They left the following afternoon, driving north towards Le Havre and spending the night at a roadside motel. They reached the port of Le Havre in the late afternoon of the following day, and by a stroke of luck managed to change their booking because of some last-minute cancellations. Ostensibly, Susan's disablement got them aboard the busy ferry, but Harriet knew without any false modesty that the unbuttoned cleavage of her green silk shirt had played no small part in persuading the taciturn port officials. They spent the night at a small hotel and embarked the following morning, reaching Southampton before noon. It took longer to disembark, but they reached London by early evening, and Harriet was more than relieved. It had been a tiring couple of days, and she was looking forward to getting back to a semblance of normality.

Her flat was in Knightsbridge, an expensive area, and it was due to Charles' connections that she got it at a reasonable rental. Nevertheless, she wouldn't have liked to live anywhere else in London, and it was useful being within walking distance of Harrods.

Susan had never stayed at the flat, and she was youthfully excited at the prospect. 'What a pretty square,' she said, looking out of the fourth floor window, and Harriet had to admit that she liked the quiet elegance of Mulhouse Close. She had come to live here almost eight years ago now, when she discovered she was pregnant and things at home became impossible.

Thinking of home reminded her of her parents, and she looked resignedly at Susan, and said: 'I suppose we'd better ring your grandmother.'

'Oh, must we?' Susan had already had a taste of her grandmother's over-anxiety when her parents died. 'Couldn't we wait until my leg's better, then tell her?'

Harriet gave a rueful shake of her head. 'Honey, I've got to let Charles know I'm back, so he won't bother coming round here to air the place for me. And I can't let Charles know, and not my mother.'

'Oh, all right.' Susan was seated on Harriet's living room couch, her leg resting comfortably on a cushion. 'But don't ask her to come up here or anything, will you? I can't stand fussing.'

Harriet went to the phone, but before ringing her mother, she rang Charles.

'Harriet!' It was good to hear his cultured tones, even if he did sound as if her calling was the last thing he had expected. 'Where are you?'

'I'm at the flat,' she told him brightly. 'Home again—with one slightly dented schoolgirl!'

'Slightly dented!' Charles gave an impatient snort. 'What are you talking about, Harriet? Why aren't you in France, lapping up that wonderful weather I hear they've been having over there?'

Harriet pulled an expressive face at her niece, and then forcing a lightness she was far from feeling, she explained: 'Susan had an accident with a scythe. She cut her leg. And, as you know, there was no bathroom as such at the house, and medical opinion seemed to suggest a more— civilised standard of plumbing.'

'Oh, Harriet!' Charles sounded half annoyed, and she couldn't think why. She had expected he would be pleased to have her back, and now. . .

'It's all right, you know,' she said, her voice revealing a little of the hurt she was feeling, 'you don't have to put up with me for another four weeks. I've got Susan staying with me here, and we can find plenty to do—'

'Harriet! Harriet, what are you talking about?' Charles sighed. 'Look, we can't talk over the phone. What are you planning to do tomorrow?'

'I'm going to rest,' said Harriet at once. 'I've been driving for three days!'

'All right!' Charles sounded thoughtful. 'The following day is Sunday. How about you and Susan joining me for lunch?'

'That sounds interesting, Charles.'

'Good. I hoped it might be. Come round here, to the apartment. Mrs Richie will have a field day having someone else to cook for. Shall we say—twelve o'clock? That will give us time to have a chat before we eat.'

'That sounds rather ominous,' murmured Harriet doubtfully, but Charles only laughed, albeit a little hollowly.

'I'll see you both on Sunday,' he said. 'Give Susan my love, and tell her to look after herself more carefully in future.'

Mrs Ingram had rather more to say on the subject of Susan. After Harriet had explained for the third time how the accident had happened, her mother sounded highly distraught.

'But imagine letting a girl of Susan's age use a scythe!' she exclaimed for the umpteenth time.

'Look, Mother, I didn't exactly *let* her use—'

'Stop splitting hairs. The fact remains, she did. She could have killed herself, Harriet. Imagine that! As if I didn't suffer enough when her mother was killed—oh, and her father, of course.'

'Of course.' Harriet met Susan's sympathetic gaze. 'Well, anyway, she's recovering rapidly—'

'You must bring her down to us at once,' declared Mrs Ingram firmly. 'It's obvious you're not fit to have charge of a girl of her age! I was doubtful about letting her go with you in the first place, particularly after. . .well,' she left that rather obvious train of thought, and started again: 'In any case, you have your own life to lead in London, and Susan's only going to be an encumbrance.'

'I've said she can stay here, Mother,' said Harriet flatly, wondering if her mother had ever felt any compassion for the granddaughter who had died, or whether that was all tied up with her mistrust of Harriet, and the disappointment *she* had been to her parents.

Susan was shifting anxiously on the couch, half aware of what was going on, and mouthing pleas to her aunt not to give in. Harriet gave her a tired smile, and tried to concentrate on what her mother was saying now.

'But what is she going to do all day while you are at the shop? Can she walk? Or is she crippled? She can't stay in the flat all day on her own!'

Harriet sighed. 'She can get about, Mother. She's not crippled. And as far as staying alone all day is concerned, she won't be. Charles doesn't expect me back at work for another month, and if I do go in to the shop, it won't be for long periods.'

'Well, I don't like it,' Mrs Ingram affirmed. 'And I'm sure your father won't either. I think we'd better come up and see Susan for ourselves, ask her what she wants to do.'

'That's up to you, of course.' Harriet shrugged her shoulders helplessly at her niece.

'Well, we can't come tomorrow. Alice and the children are coming for the day. It will have to be Sunday.'

'I'm afraid not.' Harriet was determined not

to give up her lunch with Charles. 'We're going out for lunch on Sunday.'

'You're going out? With whom? Who else knows you're back?'

Realising the cleft stick she had got herself into, Harriet quickly retreated. 'Charles— Charles was here when we got back, airing the place. He—suggested we had lunch with him on Sunday.'

Susan grinned, and her aunt pushed her chair back with a weary hand. 'If that's all, Mother—'

Mrs Ingram sounded annoyed. 'Harriet, you know your father doesn't like driving up to town after a day's work, and I'm no use on trains.'

'Well, I'm sorry. . .'

'I don't believe you are. You could have lunch with that Hockney man any day of the week. You're deliberately making obstacles. How do I know you're telling me the truth? It seems very suspicious to me that he should be there at the exact moment you arrive home.'

'I'm sorry,' said Harriet again, and she was. Her relationship with her parents, her mother in particular, had never and would never be the same again. Not since André. . .

It was strange waking up in the morning to the distant hum of traffic instead of the spirited dawn chorus of the birds she had grown used to. It was strange turning on the electric percolator instead of lighting the gas, and stepping into a tiled shower cubicle instead of dipping her face in the icy waters of the stream.

But because it was different, it had its advantages. There was shopping to do, and Mrs Burns, her own daily, to ring and ask whether she could make a special turn-out of the flat on Monday. And there were all her own personal belongings to renew acquaintance with, particularly those pieces of china and porcelain she had collected for herself over the years.

They spent a lazy day on Saturday, Susan enjoying the novelty of watching television again, and Harriet alternately loading the automatic washer with their dirty clothes, and catching up with current affairs from the newspapers. There had been another strike in the car industry, and food prices were rocketing again, but nothing earth-shattering had happened while they were away.

Charles' apartment was the top floor of a converted Victorian mansion. Large rooms with high ceilings complemented his collection of antique and reproduction furniture, and although the rooms were inclined to be a little overcrowded, the overall effect was comfortable. He lived alone, apart from an enormous black cat, which Harriet had nicknamed Perseus because of its wing-footed ability to dart among Charles' priceless *objets d'art* without knocking anything over.

His housekeeper, Mrs Richie, was there when Harriet and Susan arrived, and clucked in alarm when Susan came limping up the stairs, leaning heavily on her aunt's arm.

'Whatever next?' she exclaimed, welcoming them into the tiny entrance hall, made even tinier by the presence of a stinkwood chest which Charles had brought back from a trip to Johannesburg. 'What's wrong with good old-fashioned garden shears, I'd like to know?'

'There weren't any,' replied Harriet tolerantly, helping Susan remove her woollen coat and dropping the jacket of her rust-red trouser suit on to the chest. 'How are you, Mrs Richie? How's the rheumatism?'

Charles came to greet them in the drawing room, his plump features mirroring his pleasure, and dispelling any lingering doubts Harriet might have had about his being pleased to see her.

'Harriet, my dear,' he exclaimed, kissing both her cheeks warmly. 'And Susan! How's the invalid?'

'My leg's feeling much better, actually,' replied Susan, belying her words by sinking down with some relief into a tapestry-covered armchair, and Charles exchanged a knowing glance with Harriet before asking what they would both like to drink.

It was pleasant sitting in Charles' drawing room, long windows open to admit the maximum amount of air. It was rather a sultry day outside, and lowering clouds hid the sun, but what faint draught there was drifted into the room, and Harriet drank her gin and tonic and told herself that this was where she belonged. She was aware of Charles watching her as he conducted a conversation with Susan, and wondered why he had been so eager to speak to her. What had he to say? Did he only want to assure himself that she had got back in one piece, or was there some ulterior motive for his invitation? Not that having lunch with Charles was such an unusual occurrence; perhaps she was being super-sensitive in imagining he seemed concerned about her.

Mrs Richie's Sunday lunches were always delicious. A cold consommé was followed by roast beef and Yorkshire pudding, and Charles remarked that he had suggested the menu.

'I thought you might be glad of some good old British fare,' he said, uncorking a bottle of claret and pouring some into Harriet's glass. 'There: try that. It's part of a consignment that came up for auction last week, and I've been looking for an excuse to open a bottle.'

'Is that why you invited us here?' asked Harriet dryly, holding the ruby-coloured liquid up to the light and admiring its clarity, but Charles did not counter her teasing as she expected. Instead, he looked disconcerted, an unusual circumstance for him, and she felt even more disturbed.

Fortunately, Susan noticed nothing amiss, and after the meal was over she was quite happy to play with Perseus on the rug while Charles suggested that he and Harriet might go into his study for a private word.

'Now what is all this about?' exclaimed Harriet, as soon as the door was closed. 'Why are you behaving so strangely? What's happened while I've been away?'

'Nothing's happened while you've been away,' declared Charles firmly, indicating the chair beside his desk. 'Won't you sit down? Wandering about like that, you make me feel nervous.'

'You make me nervous!' retorted Harriet impatiently, taking the chair opposite him. 'What is it? What's going on? Why did you want to speak to me?'

'Charles sighed. 'Did you have a good holiday? What was the house like?'

'Charles!'

'My dear girl, I didn't bring you here with any intention of interrogating you. Surely I can invite my business colleague to lunch without—'

'The house was fine—eventually,' Harriet interrupted him dryly. 'But—well, the owner hadn't known it was being sold, and naturally it needed some decoration, to put it mildly.'

'Oh, dear.' Charles shook his head. 'Was it very bad?'

'We coped,' she replied briefly.

'And—and are you going back?' inquired Charles, offhandedly, but she was not deceived this time. He wanted to know.

'No,' she said flatly. 'No, I shall not be going back. I'm going to sell the house. Back to André, if he wants it.'

She watched Charles intently as she told him, and she knew her suspicions had been justified. Somehow, Charles had known André lived at Rochelac, and whether or not he had known about his owning the house, he was not shocked at hearing the other man's name mentioned.

Charles met her accusing stare with resigned eyes. 'All right,' he admitted, 'I knew Laroche lived in the area. But I didn't know he owned the house, believe me!' He paused. 'I gather you saw him again. When? What happened?'

Harriet expelled her breath in an indignant gasp. 'You dare to sit there and tell me you knew André lived near Rochelac, and then expect me to tell you what happened!' She shook her head disbelievingly. 'You've got a nerve!'

Charles leant across his desk and patted her hand, but she pulled away from him and he looked distressed. 'Harriet! Harriet, don't get upset. I only did what I thought I should.'

'What you thought you should!' she echoed dazedly. 'Charles, if you'd wanted to hurt me you couldn't have chosen a surer way!'

'Because you still care about him? I know. But, Harriet—'

'Don't "but, Harriet" me!' She got to her feet. 'I think I'd better go home, Charles, before I say something I'll regret.'

'No, wait! Don't go!' Charles was on his feet,

and appealing to her. 'Harriet, my dear, please—hear me out.'

Harriet halted in her march to the door and turned to look at him. 'It's no use, Charles...'

'Sit down again. Please!'

'Why? What is there to say?'

Charles shook his head. 'I think you ought to hear what I have to say before you jump to any—hasty conclusions.'

Harriet hesitated. 'Oh, Charles—'

'Please! Harriet, won't you even listen to what I have to tell you?'

'What have you to tell me?'

Charles sighed. 'Sit down.'

Harriet took a deep breath. 'Oh, very well. But you're wasting your time, you know.' She resumed her seat. 'There's not going to be any grand reconciliation between André and me, and I shouldn't have thought you'd want that anyway.'

Charles came to look down at her, his eyes full of compassion. 'Oh, Harriet, you can't pretend with me, my dear. I've known you too long. Would it make any difference if I told you that André wrote to me?'

CHAPTER TEN

THE room was very quiet. Harriet could even hear the ticking of the French ormolu clock on the mantelpiece—or was that her heart beating audibly in her ears?

'Wh-what did you say?' she got out at last, staring up at Charles uncomprehendingly. '*André* wrote to *you*! When?'

Charles patted her shoulder, and then draped one of his short legs over the corner of the desk near her, swinging his foot rather absently. 'Well, it was about six months ago, actually,' he replied thoughtfully. 'Soon after Christmas, I believe. I know the Jennings exhibition was on at the time—'

'Oh, never mind the Jennings exhibition,' exclaimed Harriet frustratedly. 'Why didn't you tell me? Why did he write to you?'

Charles folded his hands together. 'His wife had just died. Did you know about that?'

Harriet nodded. 'He told me, yes.'

Charles looked surprised. 'But that must have—that is—doesn't that mean anything to you?'

Harriet held up her head. 'Only that while he was—was seeing me, his wife was suffering

191

from some incurable disease!' she said tremulously.

Charles stared at her. '*Some* incurable disease!' he echoed blankly. 'Don't you know what it was?'

Harriet moved her head restlessly. 'No. And I don't want to know. Charles,' she looked up, 'where is all this leading? Are you trying to tell me that he knew I was buying the house all along?'

'No, no!' Charles spoke impatiently. 'Look, I think it would be easier if you told me how you came to meet André again.'

Harriet made a gesture of dismissal. 'Why?'

'Won't you tell me? I'd like to know.'

Harriet shook her head helplessly. 'If you must know, he was at the house, the day we arrived. He'd only just learned it had been sold, or so he said. He was—cleaning it out.'

'Was he—shocked to see you?'

Harriet frowned. 'Come to think of it, I guess I was more shocked than he was.' She stared belligerently at him. 'But then of course I would be, wouldn't I? I didn't know he'd been corresponding with you!'

Charles nodded. 'So—go on. What happened?'

'Not a lot. He offered me my money back, actually. He couldn't do much else, I suppose. The house was in a deplorable state.'

'But you didn't take it.'

'No.' She coloured then. 'Oh, not because of

him. But Susan would have been so disappointed and I'd never have been able to negotiate another sale in the time. . .'

'So you stayed on.'

'Until Susan had her accident, yes.'

Charles digested this thoughtfully. 'Did you see Laroche again? I suppose you must have done.'

'Why should you suppose that?' she flared.

'Well, I hardly expect he would blurt out the news of his wife's death in the first few minutes he spoke with you,' replied Charles dryly. 'Or did he?'

'No.' Harriet looked down at the creases in her trousers. 'No, we met several times, actually.'

'I see.'

'As a matter of fact, he helped me to get Susan to the hospital. When she had her accident. He was very—considerate.'

Charles studied her downbent head. 'But you're not seeing him again?'

'No.'

'Why not?'

'Charles!' She lifted her head to stare indignantly at him. 'You may be my employer, but you're not my keeper. Besides, I always thought you disapproved of him.'

Charles sighed now. 'I did. Until I saw what you were becoming.'

'What do you mean?'

He leant forward and took one of her hands

in both of his. 'My dear girl, don't get upset about this, but you know what you've become as well as I do: a career girl, first and foremost.'

'What's wrong with that?'

'Nothing—within reason. But you don't behave reasonably. You seldom go out, you've made working your primary objective in life— and you won't let any man near you!'

Harriet would have drawn away from him then, but he kept hold of her hand, and she gazed at him defensively. 'What you mean is, I've grown up,' she declared unsteadily. 'Just because I'm not the silly, impressionable girl I used to be—'

'But you are,' said Charles firmly. 'Oh, not silly, but impressionable, yes. You've grown a shell, that's all. You think you can hide from life. Well, you can't, Harriet, and the sooner you realise it the better.'

'Is that what André told you?'

'No. No, of course not. I told you what André said. He told me his wife had died. He asked me how you were, and whether you were happy. I never replied.'

Harriet gasped. 'You didn't?'

'No.' Charles shook his head. 'What could I say? Could I tell him that in my opinion you were wasting your life? Or should I have lied and told him you were a happy and contented girl?'

'I am happy and contented. Or I was!'

'You were living in a backwater!' declared

Charles fiercely, releasing her hand to get to his feet.

'I have friends. . .'

'Not close friends. Apart from myself, of course. I do count myself as your friend, whatever happens.'

Harriet pressed her palms together. 'So you—decided to send me to France. . .'

'After Laroche wrote to me, I knew I had to do something. I knew you liked France, particularly after that trip we made to Limoges, so I started putting out feelers, making enquiries about buying property in the Dordogne.' He paused. 'I influenced you, I know, but you must admit you were eager.' Harriet nodded, and he finished: 'Then your sister and her husband were killed and—well, the rest you know.'

Harriet shook her head disbelievingly. 'So coincidences don't always happen.'

'It was a coincidence that André should own the house you chose to buy.'

'I suppose so.' Harriet expelled her breath softly.

'How does he look?'

'André?' She shivered. 'Older. Harder.'

'Tougher?'

'I suppose you could say that.'

'He's had a hard time. It's bound to have taken its toll.'

'He's had a hard time,' Harriet echoed shortly. 'His wife's had a hard time, too.'

Charles frowned. 'Medical bills cost money.

It had to come from somewhere. That day we met him in the St Germain salerooms, he was selling some of the Rochefort silver. I should imagine everything's gone by now, and they owned some beautiful things. From riches to rags; a paradox, wouldn't you say?'

'Don't try to make me feel sorry for him!' she exclaimed scornfully. 'His wife couldn't help being ill.'

'No,' agreed Charles mildly. 'And he couldn't help the fact that she spent the last twelve years of her life in a mental institution!'

'*What*!' It was as well that Harriet was sitting down when he told her, or her legs would not have supported her. 'Charles, what are you saying?'

'I'm saying that Laroche's wife was sick, mentally sick. She was an hysterical woman when he married her, and she should never have had any children. She never fully recovered after their son was born.'

'How do you know all this?' Harriet cried desperately. 'André can't have told you!'

'No,' Charles agreed. 'All he told me was that his wife had died in hospital after a prolonged illness. Curiosity—call it what you will—made me make enquiries. The Rochefort family are not entirely unknown in that area of France.'

'Oh, God!' Harriet buried her face in her hands. Charles' words had explained so many things, not least that letter she had received from André after their weekend in Paris, informing her oh, so politely that he could never marry her because he was married already, and there was no question of a divorce.

Charles' arm encircled her shoulders. 'I'm sorry, my dear, but I had to tell you. You had to know. It was only right.'

Harriet lifted an anguished face. 'But—but what can I do? I never knew. I never realised. I just thought—' She broke off abruptly. 'If only I'd known. . .'

Charles' eyes narrowed. 'Yes? What would you have done?'

Harriet's lips quivered. 'I don't know. I don't know.'

'Did you tell him about the baby?'

She nodded.

'What did he say?'

She shook her head. 'I think—I think he was shattered.'

'With good reason.' Charles made a protesting sound. 'Poor man! He's had more than his share of misery, I should think.'

Harriet gulped. 'He thinks I hate him.'

'But you don't.'

She shook her head. 'I've tried to. I used to think I did. Then when I saw him again. . .'

'. . .you knew you didn't?'

She nodded. 'I love him, Charles. I think I always have.'

'Does he love you?'

'I don't know.' She stared into space. 'I think it's probably too late for that.'

'Why?'

'Oh, Charles, emotion can't be turned on and off like a tap. Maybe if I'd known. . .'

'Then it's my fault,' said Charles heavily. 'I should have told you.'

'Don't be silly.' She looked at him through tearful eyes. 'You weren't supposed to know. André should have told me himself.'

A knock at the study door signalled the end of their conversation. Susan poked her head round, and looked anxious when she saw Harriet had been crying.

'What's the matter?' she exclaimed. 'Mr Hockney! Are you angry with Harriet?'

'No, no, no.' Charles went forward, giving Harriet time to pull herself together. 'We've been talking about a—mutual friend, someone who's had rather a lot of bad luck lately. I'm afraid your aunt got rather upset, that's all.'

On Monday Harriet went to the shop in the morning. She assured herself that Susan would be content for a couple of hours with a jigsaw puzzle Charles had lent her, and then took a bus to Kensington High Street.

The little bell rang as she opened the door and Charles himself appeared from his room at the back. 'Harriet!' he exclaimed. 'I didn't expect you to come in today.'

Harriet closed the door behind her. 'No, I know you didn't. But so long as Susan's leg is in stitches, there's not a lot we can do, and I'd rather be working than sitting doing nothing.'

If Charles understood the reasons for that statement, he made no comment, and she was grateful. There had been enough soul-pourings yesterday. Today, she wanted to take up the threads of her life and see whether it was possible to put what had happened out of her mind. She could never go to André, after the way she had treated him, and it seemed unlikely that he would come to her.

Her mother rang on Monday evening to see how Susan was, and Harriet let her speak to her grand-daughter. Susan was less chary of offending her than she was, and a child could get away with so much more than an adult.

But when Susan came off the phone she was looking thoughtful and Harriet raised her eyebrows inquisitively when she heaved a sigh before sinking down on to the couch again.

'Is something wrong?' Harriet was sensitive to her niece's moods by now, and Susan definitely looked troubled.

Susan lay back against the cushions, and pulled a face. 'No.'

'Oh, come on.' Harriet wasn't having that. 'What did she say?'

Susan sniffed. 'Nothing much.' Then she hunched her shoulders. 'Aunt Harriet, couldn't we go down and see Grandma? I think she's very worried about my leg.'

Harriet stared at her incredulously. 'You *want* to go to Guildford?'

Susan flushed. 'Well, just for the day, of course. It wouldn't be so bad, would it? I mean, you'd like to see your mother, wouldn't you?'

Harriet tried to be patient. 'Are you bored here? Is that what's wrong? If you are, just say so, love. I don't mind. I realise it's not the same as being on holiday, but till your leg heals, there's not a lot we can do.'

Susan quickly shook her head. 'I'm not bored! I like it here. But—well, Grandma says she's got me a present.'

'Ah!' Harriet began to understand. 'Well, why didn't you say so?'

Susan looked uncomfortable. 'It's a dog.'

'A *dog*!' Harriet stared at her aghast. Then she nodded her head cynically. 'A dog, eh? Well, well! Who'd have thought it?'

'What do you mean?'

'Your grandmother used not to allow animals in the house. Obviously, she's prepared to make an exception in your case.'

'Well, it will be fun, won't it?' exclaimed Susan eagerly. 'I mean, I'll be able to take it for walks and things, when my leg's better, and Grandma says I can train it myself.'

Harriet draped one arm over the back of her chair. 'And who is going to look after it while you're here?' she enquired softly.

Now Susan looked perturbed. 'Can't I bring it back with me?'

'I'm afraid not. Dogs aren't allowed in the flats.'

'They're not!' Susan looked dismayed.

'No.' And your grandmother knows that, Harriet added silently.

Susan frowned. 'Oh, dear. Well, Grandma won't want to take care of it for another month.'

'She shouldn't have got it until term-time,' remarked Harriet reasonably.

'She said she thought I'd have more time to train him in the holidays.'

Harriet rose to her feet. 'There you are, then. What are you going to do?'

Susan sighed, looking wretched, and her aunt took pity on her. After all, it wasn't her fault that Mrs Ingram was so determined to have her own way.

'I think perhaps you'd better go back to Grandma's,' she said gently. 'She's right. You will have more time for a dog in the holidays, and I think it's a splendid idea, having a pet of your own.'

'Do you really think so?' Susan looked relieved. 'I don't want to let you down. . . .'

'Honey, you're not letting me down. I've had my holiday now. I'd as soon get back to work. You go home and enjoy yourself.'

The day spent at her parents' home in Guildford was not an easy one. Harriet had to take Susan's medical notes with her so that they could be passed on to the local hospital, and she had to explain how the dressing on her leg should be changed and in so doing exhibited the coarse line of stitches to her mother's horrified gaze.

'Oh, you poor child!' Mrs Ingram exclaimed with feeling, and her exaggerated sympathy almost had Susan in tears.

But the Labrador puppy was a great success, and Harriet drove away with some relief in the late afternoon, leaving Susan romping on the hearthrug with the playful animal.

Fortunately Susan had not been long enough at the flat for Harriet to get used to having her around, and within a couple of days she was back into the old routine. But she didn't sleep at all well, and because she had only herself to cater for, she didn't eat too well either. Her waking moments were plagued with the realisation that she had destroyed the only chance of happiness she was ever likely to have, and if she could have lived those weeks in France over again, knowing what she knew now, how differently she would have behaved.

There were times, of course, when she contemplated going back to Rochelac. She had not yet put the house in the estate agent's hands, and she pictured. André's surprise when he found she was living in it once more. But then she would imagine how she might feel if he treated her as she had treated him, and the craven spirit inside her refused to invite such a rebuff. It was no use. She simply did not have the gall to go back and ask for something she had been so unwilling to grant.

Then one morning, something unexpected happened. She was attending to a customer when the shop door opened and Paul Laroche came in. She had looked up automatically, but her eyes widened in astonishment—and apprehension—when she saw André's son. Dressed in jeans and a shabby cotton jerkin, he was no different from a thousand other youths one might see in the street, but he was certainly not the usual type of customer they served.

Charles, aware that Harriet was occupied, came out of the back room to offer his assistance, and then frowned when he saw the boy. 'Yes?' he asked abruptly, and Harriet, trying to concentrate on what she was doing, heard the censure in his voice. She guessed Charles imagined he had some ulterior motive for coming into the shop, and he would try to get rid of him.

'Excuse me,' she said, and leaving her customer examining a pair of Georgian candleholders, she interposed herself between the two men. Charles looked at her impatiently, but she turned to him pointedly and said: 'Do you know André's son, Charles?'

Charles looked stunned, and leaving him to recover, she turned to Paul. She noticed how much thinner the boy was looking, and he seemed to have lost the arrogance she had noticed that day in Rochelac. But perhaps that scene he had witnessed with his father had changed the way he felt towards her.

'Are you looking for me?' she asked, trying to speak casually, wondering with a sick feeling whether anything had happened to his father.

'Yes.' Paul exchanged a polite smile with Charles, who had gathered himself again, and then concentrated his attention on Harriet. 'Can I talk to you?'

'You can use my office,' offered Charles, but noticing Paul's agitation, Harriet decided against it.

'We'll go and have some coffee together,' she said, squeezing Charles' arm in passing, so he should not feel slighted, and leaving him to attend to their customer, she followed Paul outside.

It was a sunny morning, and they walked towards the park, stopping on the way at Harriet's suggestion to buy a couple of tins of Coke and two doughnuts. Paul attacked his doughnut as if he was starving, and watching him Harriet felt a pang.

'When did you last have any food?' she demanded, and Paul's face suffused with colour.

'Yesterday,' he declared defensively, but he couldn't meet her eyes.

With a sigh, Harriet thrust her doughnut into his hand, and although he made a feeble protest, he ate it just the same. They found a seat in the park, and then Harriet turned to him urgently, her eyes revealing her concern.

'So?' she said. 'What are you doing in London?'

Paul tugged the ring-fastener off his Coke, and drank from the can before answering. Then, with a resigned shrug, he said: 'I ran away.'

'You what!' Harriet was horrified. 'When?' She paused. 'Why?'

Paul shook his head. 'It must be ten—maybe eleven days ago now,' he answered. 'The night I—well, the night I saw you and Papa!'

'Oh, no!' Harriet stared at him aghast. 'But, Paul—'

'Do not distress yourself. You are not to blame. I should have believed—' He broke off shrugging. 'But there it was, and I ran—' He drank from the can again, and Harriet tried desperately to think what to do.

'Does your father know where you are?' she exclaimed.

Paul shook his head once more. 'I think not.'

'But he must be half out of his mind with worry!'

'Yes.'

Paul sounded thoughtful, and she burst out fretfully: 'Don't you care?'

'Do you?' he countered candidly, and now she flushed.

'I—we're not talking about me.'

'Are we not?' Paul's jaw jutted. 'But you have run away, too, have you not?'

Harriet stared at him. 'How did you know I was back in London?'

'You were not at the house. Where else could you be?'

Harriet was confused. 'Explain this to me, please! What were you doing at the house?'

Paul sighed. 'Very well. The night—the night I saw you with my father, I spent in the chateau. I knew my father would not think of looking for me there, and I needed time to think. The next day I went to my aunt in Sarlat. She did not suspect anything was wrong, but I knew I could not stay there for long, so I came back to Roch-elac. I wanted to see you, to talk to you. But you had gone. That was when I decided to come to England.'

Harriet shook her head bewilderedly. 'But do you have a passport?' He shook his head. 'And how have you lived?'

Paul made a sweeping gesture. 'I—borrowed some money from my aunt, and how do you say it?—hitched a ride?' Harriet nodded, and he went on: 'I managed to get to Dijon with a wagon driver, and when he was not looking, I stowed away.'

He sounded quite proud when he said this, but Harriet was horrified, and the paleness of her face prompted him to ask if she was feeling all right.

'I'm all right,' she protested. 'But, Paul, how do you think your father is feeling right now?'

Paul hunched his shoulders, and she noticed how much narrower they were. 'I do not know. Perhaps he does not care.'

'You know that's not true, Paul,' she cried. 'He—he went after you that night. He wanted to try and explain. . .' And Paul's disappearance also explained why André had not come back, she thought weakly.

'So. . .' Paul sighed. Then: 'Why did you run away?'

'I didn't run away,' Harriet denied, although she knew she had. 'I brought Susan home.'

'But my father cares about you, does he not? Do you not care about him?'

Harriet looked drained. 'Yes,' she said frankly, 'I care about him. Is that what you wanted to hear?'

Paul frowned. 'I wanted to come to London, but my father would never let me. I really made you the excuse.'

'I see.'

'But I want to go home now.'

Harriet hid her relief. 'How did you find me?'

Paul half smiled. 'I found your mother in the telephone directory, and used my last two pence to ring you. But another woman answered. A Mrs Burns, yes? She told me you were at work, and here I am.'

Harriet sighed now. 'Oh, Paul!'

'It has been quite an adventure, no?'

'How am I going to get you back to France? You don't have a passport!'

Paul looked at her appealingly. 'You will think of something, I am sure,' he said, and she couldn't help wondering whether all this talk of seeing her again had been designed to gain her sympathy. After all, he had said he wanted to come to London, and perhaps it had not lived

up to his expectations. Whatever, she owed it to
André to get his son home again, and the only
person she knew who might know a way was
Charles.

CHAPTER ELEVEN

IT was late when Harriet got home from Charles' apartment. It had been a long evening spent with Paul while Charles contacted various friends he had in the Foreign Office, and managed to explain matters satisfactorily to the proper authorities. It was being arranged that Paul should fly back in the morning, and a car laid on to take him the rest of the way home. Charles had suggested the boy spent the night at his apartment, rather than Harriet's, for obvious reasons, and she was only too pleased to delegate the responsibiltiy to someone else. Even so, she was weary when she reached Mulhouse Close, a weariness that intensified when she recognised her father's car parked outside the block of flats. What now? she thought defeatedly, unable to imagine what he could be doing here at this hour.

The car was empty, and guessing the caretaker had let him in, Harriet took the lift up to the fourth floor. But as she emerged into the shadowy corridor, a dark figure straightened from the wall beside her door, and she had to put her hand to her mouth to stifle a cry. But even in the gloom she had recognised André, and she stared at him hungrily, half afraid her longing for him had created this manifestation.

'You are late.'

His cool words dispelled the illusion of unreality, and hot colour stained her cheeks. What was he doing here? Had he come in search of Paul, and if so, why should he assume she would know where he was?

Now she fumbled in her bag for her key, and taking it out, inserted it rather inaccurately in the lock and pushed open the door.

'Will you come in?' she asked, going ahead to switch on the light, and André inclined his head and followed her into the narrow hall of the flat.

Harriet walked into the living room, shedding the jacket of her cream trouser suit, aware that her hair was probably tumbled and that there was a stain of metal polish on the sleeve of her silk shirt which she had spilt during the distracting afternoon she had spent. André came to the living room door and looked at her. He was wearing a grey lounge suit, his linen immaculate in the artificial light, and Harriet felt her senses stirring irresistibly. He looked so haggard and weary, his eyes as guarded as the expression he was wearing.

'I suppose you're looking for Paul,' she began, her voice slightly higher than normal, and then gasped when he crossed the room in a couple of strides to take her by the shoulders.

'*Paul*!' he echoed grimly. 'You have seen Paul?'

His eyes glittered strangely now, and

Harriet felt bewildered. 'I—well, yes—'

'And you did not think to let me know?' He released her so roughly that she almost lost her balance. 'But of course! Why should you? It is nothing to do with you is it?'

Harriet stared at him blankly, and then put out a restraining hand as he would have turned away. 'Wait, André! I haven't had time to let you know. I saw him for the first time today!'

'What?' He turned to stare disbelievingly at her.

'It's true! I swear.' Harriet's fingers sought the open neckline of her shirt. 'He—he came to the shop this morning.'

André expelled his breath heavily and then raked unsteady fingers through his hair. 'I have searched everywhere for him,' he muttered, half to himself. 'How in the name of all that is sacred did he get to England?'

Harriet told him: 'He hitch-hiked to Dijon and stowed away on the ferry.'

'Dear God!' André sounded stunned. 'So—where is he?'

'He's spending the night at Charles' apartment.'

'Hockney?'

'Yes.' She moved her shoulders awkwardly. 'I've just come from there. That's why I'm so late.'

'And is he all right?'

'Paul? Yes, I think so.' She paused. 'He wants

to go home. Charles has been trying to arrange it.'

André looked as though he found it all rather hard to take in, and Harriet gestured towards the couch, realising as she did so that if André had not come here looking for Paul, she didn't know why he had come.

'Please,' she murmured, 'won't you sit down? I—I'll make some coffee.'

André shook his head rather dazedly, and then stepped towards her. 'I—must apologise—' he began, but she made a deprecating gesture. 'There's no need. . .'

'Very well.' He drew in his breath. 'I am sorry if I frightened you, but this has been quite a week for me.' He sighed, and she saw the grim agony in his eyes. 'First Paul, then you! I am surprised I am still sane.'

'Oh, André. . .' Harriet quivered. 'What are you doing here?'

'You must know,' he told her heavily. 'It is late, and I am tired, but I had to see you. I have been waiting here almost two hours.'

Harriet tugged distractedly at a strand of her hair. 'The car—the car outside; it's Daddy's, isn't it?'

'Your father's? Yes.' His eyes darkened, and her knees wobbled. 'But do not ask me to explain—not yet. Just let me look at you.'

'André. . .' It was a protest, and yet nothing could have prevented her from going to him and taking his face between her two hands and reaching up to touch the corner of his mouth with her own.

'You left me,' he breathed harshly. 'Not once, but many times. Why do I keep coming back?'

Harriet licked her lips, her tongue knowingly provocative. 'You tell me,' she whispered, noticing a muscle jerking at his jawline.

'I wrote to Charles,' he said roughly. 'Did he tell you? He never replied, and I learned to live with the belief that you were married. And then you appeared, like some avenging angel, and destroyed my peace of mind once and for all.'

'Oh, André, you have to forgive me. . .'

'Forgive you?' He shook his head bitterly. 'For what? For running out on me when I needed you most? Or for carrying my child and not letting me know you were pregnant?'

Harriet trembled. 'I couldn't let you know.'

'You got my letter, did you not? You knew you could reach me through the saleroom.'

'André, you were married! You said there was no question of—of a divorce.'

He uttered an oath. 'I know, I know. But you should have told me.' He sighed. 'The situation—was not like you think. I know you think I treated my wife very badly, and possibly you are right. But she did not know. She never knew.'

He turned abruptly away from her, running a tired hand round the back of his neck. 'She was sick, yes,' he said in a muffled voice. 'Mentally sick. She spent the last twelve years of her life in a mental institution!'

'I know.'

He glanced round at her. 'You *know*!'

'Charles—Charles made enquiries. After you wrote to him.'

'And you knew!' His face was tortured.

'Not until a few days ago.' She went to him eagerly. 'André! André, I thought you didn't care! That you had never cared!'

'Oh, I cared,' he murmured, running unsteady hands over her hair, his fingers lingering against her nape. 'But you were so young and beautiful. And I could not let you waste your youth waiting for me—'

'It wouldn't have been wasted,' she protested. 'If only you'd told me!'

He sighed. 'I could not do that. I guessed if I had you might have wanted to wait, but then you would have got bored, and I knew I could not bear that.'

'Oh, André!'

'Yes. . .' His eyes dropped to her mouth. 'Yes, Harriet. . .'

Her arms slid round his waist, under his jacket, and his mouth sought hers with probing insistence. His tongue traced the outline of her lips, and then as they parted, his mouth took hard possession of hers. Without restraint, their kisses were deep and satisfying, and Harriet was weak and clinging to him when he pulled her down on to the couch beside him.

'We have to talk,' he muttered, when her lips turned against his neck, her hands seeking the buttons of his shirt. 'Do you not wish to know why your father's car is outside?'

Harriet curled herself against him. 'If you must tell me. . .'

His lips moved lazily. 'Do you not wish to know that I came to ask you to go back with me?' Her eyes widened. 'That I told your parents that I want to marry you?'

'André!' She knelt beside him, staring at him eagerly. 'You came back to ask me that?'

'That night—at the house—before Paul interrupted us. You cannot deny you wanted me as much as I wanted you.'

Harriet's cheeks turned slightly pink. 'I don't deny it.'

He sighed impatiently. 'Yet you ran away.'

'I had to get away. I was ashamed. I didn't trust you, and I didn't trust myself.'

'Oh, Harriet, if you had only let me explain. . .'

'I know.' She raised his hand to her lips and then held it against her cheek. 'Instead, Charles did the explaining.'

'Thank God for Charles!'

André leant over her, his hands intimately caressing, and all resistance went out of her. For a long moment there was silence in the apartment, and then with a ragged protest, André dragged himself away from her.

'You said something about some coffee,' he

muttered huskily, and with a smug little smile, Harriet fastened her shirt again and got to her feet.

André followed her to the kitchen door and stood leaning against the doorpost, watching her. He had shed his jacket, and his shirt was unbuttoned, and Harriet thought she had never loved him so much as she did right now.

'Your mother was most surprised to see me,' he remarked, and Harriet looked up from grinding the coffee beans.

'What did she say?'

'She asked me why I wanted to see you. I think your father knew.'

'But why did you go to Guildford?'

He shrugged. 'The shop was closed, and it was barely five o'clock—'

'I know. Charles closed early because of Paul.'

'Ah, yes, Paul.' André sounded thoughtful; then he went on: 'I remembered your parents lived in Guildford, so I caught the train there.'

'And Daddy lent you his car to come back here?'

'When I had assured him my intentions were honourable.'

'And are they?' she teased.

'Not right at this moment,' he admitted softly, coming to slide his arms around her from behind. 'Hmm, that feels good.'

Harriet moulded herself against him. 'What about Paul?'

André sighed. 'What about him?'

'He knows about us.'

'He saw us together, you mean?'

'No.' She shifted restlessly. 'I—I told him I—cared about you.'

'Keep still,' he muttered thickly. Then: 'What did he say?'

'I don't think he was surprised.'

'No, he would not be. The night—the night I came to invite you to the lodge for supper, I told both him and Louise how I felt about you.'

'Oh, André!'

'I do not think he believed me. Perhaps that was why he came to the house as he did. *N'importe*, he disappeared that night and I have not seen him since.'

'He told me.' Harriet twisted round in his arms. 'He said he spent the first night in the chateau, and the following day he went to his aunt in Sarlat.'

'My sister—yes, I heard about that,' André nodded. 'Harriet, I have spent the past week looking for him. I wanted to come after you at once, but my conscience told me I must find Paul first. At last I could wait no longer, and what did I find? *You* had found my son!'

'He found me,' corrected Harriet gently, and told him how Paul had discovered her address.

'And now?' he said softly, holding her closer.

The percolator began to bubble in the background, but Harriet barely noticed it. 'That—that's up to you.'

'I want you to come back to France with me—
with me and Paul.'

'If that's what you want.'

'*Chérie*, you know what I want. What I have
always wanted.' Then he frowned. 'But first I
must tell you about Irène.'

'Irène? That was your wife?'

'Yes.' He sighed. 'I will not insult your intelligence by telling you I never cared for her. I did.
She was a beautiful woman, too, and I was very
young.' He paused. 'Only later did the flaw
become evident—'

She put her fingers over her lips. 'You don't
have to tell me. . .'

'I want to,' he said, turning his lips against
her palm.

'So much has changed since I married Irène.
The Rocheforts lost much of their wealth at the
time of the Revolution, but once we were not
poor. Now I am only a farmer—'

'Do you think I care?'

'I think you love me. . .'

'I do.'

'And I adore you. Is that enough?'

'What more could we want?'

'There is one thing I must tell you—the
specialists who attended Irène at the time of
her—breakdown were of the opinion that pregnancy had enhanced her condition. . .'

'It doesn't matter, darling.'

'It does.' He looked down at her passionately.
'I could not bear anything to happen to you, and

pregnancies do not seem fortunate things for me. Irène had a very difficult time, and you—you lost your baby.'

'My baby was perfectly healthy,' she declared fervently. André, what are you saying now? That we shouldn't have any children?'

'Perhaps.'

'Try and stop me,' she whispered huskily, and with a muffled groan he buried his face in her hair.

'I do not think I can,' he confessed, and a small smile touched the lips she lifted to his.

MILLS & BOON

Anne Mather

COLLECTOR'S EDITION

If you have missed any of the previously published titles in the Anne Mather Collector's Edition, you may order them by sending a cheque or postal order (please do not send cash) made payable to Harlequin Mills & Boon Ltd. for £2.99 per book plus 50p per book postage and packing. Please send your order to: Anne Mather Collector's Edition, P.O. Box 236, Croydon, Surrey, CR9 3RU (EIRE: Anne Mather Collector's Edition, P.O. Box 4546, Dublin 24).

1 JAKE HOWARD'S WIFE
2 SCORPIONS' DANCE
3 CHARADE IN WINTER
4 A FEVER IN THE BLOOD
5 WILD ENCHANTRESS
6 SPIRIT OF ATLANTIS

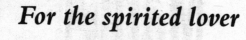

NEW YORK TIMES
BESTSELING AUTHOR

Anne Mather

Dangerous Temptation

He was desperate to remember... Jake wasn't sure
why he'd agreed to take his twin brother's place on
the flight to London. But when he awakens in hospital
after the crash, he can't even remember his own
name or the beautiful woman who watches him so
guardedly. Caitlin. His wife.

She was desperate to forget... Her husband seems
like a stranger to Caitlin—a man who assumes there
is love when none exists. He is totally different—like
the man she'd thought she had married. Until his
memory returns.
And with it, a danger that threatens them all.

"Ms. Mather has penned a wonderful romance."
—Romantic Times

MIRA   **AVAILABLE NOW IN PAPERBACK**